THE AFFINITY BETWEEN US

— • ☾ • —

A Short Story Collection

Melissa Sweeney

This is a work of fiction.
Names, characters, places, or incidents are either products of the author's imagination or are used fictitiously. Any resemblance of people, living or dead, is entirely fictional.

ISBN 979-8-3492-9546-1 (pbk)
ISBN 979-8-3492-9547-8 (ebook)
All rights reserved © 2025 Melissa Sweeney
Cover art © Melissa Sweeney

THE AFFINITY BETWEEN US
Prologue

———————◆ ☾ ◆———————

Maïmoú never understood the meaning of time. Sundials and obelisks, analog clocks and hourglasses. The world got dark and then light. The Sun and Moon did their dance. That was all she needed to know.

But her time worked differently now. She no longer had shadows or clocks or technology to tell her how much time was passing. This dark prison she'd found herself in was like a dream, or nightmare: her Void, a lifeless state filled only with Greco ruins and emptiness. Nothingness.

They mocked her, for every day, every year, every *century* that crept by, they never changed. They didn't crumble or wither. They were locked in time and forgotten about in the back rooms of life.

For the first hundred years, she hadn't gone insane. She couldn't move her broken body, but if she could, she'd prance around and boast about how accomplished she was as a Deity. She'd handled her isolation so well, even Sabah would've been surprised. When Maïmoú eventually freed herself, she'd walk the earth like a celebrity among her beloved fans.

Whatever had happened to her, it'd left her comatose, essentially, a coma patient with the unfortunate fate of semi-consciousness. She couldn't remember exactly what'd happened to her before she wound up here. She'd been fighting with Shào, as always, then there was smoke, then a bright light that'd made her body go limp. She remembered lots of crying and screaming, a woman's voice. What sucked was that these memories faded with time, so the more time she spent thinking about it, the farther away the minute details became.

Despite the situation, Maïmoú wasn't scared. She didn't fear anything, just like her humans. Whatever they might've "feared" was just anger masquerading as a more palatable emotion. You weren't afraid of pain, you were angry that something dared to hurt you. You hated those who belittled your power. You hated their simple lives.

Whoever had done this to her, whoever had ruined her progress with humanity, would pay. She'd made that promise the moment she could think clearly, and she swore to keep it until the Sun stopped rising.

One day.
One day.
One day.

Between a time she couldn't place and now, she'd discovered herself. She was more aware of her surroundings. She could keep track of time by etching it into the walls of her mind. One tally for every time she awoke.

She stargazed. Every other day, her eyes would open to the black sky above her. It pulsed with energy, splattering the darkness with constellations that glowed in deep purples. She saw patterns, roadwork in the sky. She could no longer levitate towards them, but she could reach her thin arm up to them, wanting.

Those wants turned to a need, then a craving. It grew ever so slowly, her starvation for more, to take something she'd fought for.

Once she grasped it, that little flame in need of oxygen, her warped sense of time shifted. She could now count down the seconds which turned to minutes. The days passed by slower because she was now living every single day.

On a peculiarly vivid day, when all of her senses were overreacting to the feelings of nothingness, she felt a twitch in the air. She'd been up against a broken column, head slumped into her knees and staring into the nothingness, when she saw it.

There was a light at the horizon line. It wasn't like the starlight that flickered above her. This was tangible, a light at the end of her dark tunnel.

Her knees pushed herself up. Her neck arched to get her upper half moving. Hands that hadn't moved properly in centuries clawed into the nothingness she now knew was the floor. Forwards, forwards.

Her fingers tangled through tiny wisps on the ground. They were so thin, they could've been her own matted hair, but her hair hadn't been brushed in eons. Unsure of what was happening, Maïmoú grasped onto the strings like life preservers and tugged herself up.

Her voice, a sound now foreign to her, ripped out through her tiny body. "Let...me...*out*!" she bellowed into her Void.

The darkness screeched back in harrowing screams. She screamed louder, harder, turning monstrous. "Let me out!"

She clawed at the ground, fingers tangling in the strings. Her echoing voice dipped in and out of her ears until all of it was sucked away in one swift gulp. She floated for a second in her nothingness before being thrown out through a blinding window of light.

She hit something hard. Her senses exploded like bombs in her face. Her cheek grated against a cold surface, and she landed facefirst in cold mud. Her ears were buzzing like she had bees inside her.

It wasn't bees. It was rain. The soft gentleness you'd find outside, cold and damp. She was in an overgrown forest slick with wet leaves and soggy soil. It freshened the world with sounds and smells that enhanced the colors of the world.

She turned her body through the mud, unaware that she was screaming as loudly as her broken lungs would heave out. She felt like she was on fire. She was trapped in an oven with the red-hot irons branding her skin and melting her bones—the burn of being alive.

She laughed through her pain, cackling like a storybook witch. She'd done it. She'd defied Fate and fought her way back into freedom. And living was painful and heartbreaking and of *course*, it was raining, because why wouldn't it be? She was Maïmoú of Athens. Her life was packaged in heartbreak.

And nothing would ever feel as great as this moment.

She wanted to stand, but her body disobeyed. Without admitting it aloud, she was too hurt to move. So there she lay, struggling like a wingless bird, as the world received its rain. It wasn't even needed—from the soil's texture, it must've rained frequently here. Tropical birds cawed around her. She heard a four-legged creature prowling in the woods. At least life had continued on while she was gone.

What did it look like, the world? How far had humanity advanced in her absence? Were they still as powerful and dominant as she'd left them? What about the Others? What'd become of them, of Shào?

Gradually, painfully, Maïmoú struggled to sit up. A string was being tugged in her heart, guiding her onto the right path.

She fell into a tree, snapping it and dropping it into a static pond. She plummeted knee-deep into watery mud. As she gasped for breath, she caught her reflection in the watery mud.

Her hair had grown. That was all she registered before her anger slapped the puddle into ripples. When she'd been great, she didn't like looking into mirrors. Now, she wouldn't be able to stomach it.

She pushed back her wet hair. She needed to get a hold of herself. Focus. She could walk. She had to.

She looked up. Through the droplets of rain clinging to her eyelashes, she saw a string. It was tied around trees and over falling logs. It was thin, barely aglow through the haze of rain, but she saw it, felt it. It began inside her chest, tugging her heartstrings.

She clutched her chest, suddenly breathless without the need to breathe. Her desire to be freed hadn't come from her alone. She had no control over herself. Just like with every Deity, all of their wants and needs stemmed from very small, very fragile living beings.

She dug her shoeless feet into the mud and hoisted herself up. Her vision went dark around the corners as she focused on the red string. She'd had one string like this before, two, technically, though they were so intertwined, they appeared as one.

She grasped onto the string, and from it came apart another. Two red strings of fate, tied to her and two others.

She took off, hitting every rock and stump and pond in this nameless forest. Getting on all fours, she tracked the red strings for a half-mile before breaking into a meadow.

She didn't recognize the city. It wasn't anything remarkable—it had a few skyscrapers in its business district and palm trees indicating they were close to the equator. The meadow was overgrown and the trees still had berries on them, meaning the people weren't poverty-stricken. What caught her eye was the tall, all-encompassing wall that surrounded the world. It shot up at least 1,000 feet. It was a thick, gray slate of concrete with darker stone etched into it every quarter mile. From the age and weather of the rock, it looked like it'd been there for centuries.

She turned in a full circle, questioning where she was, what'd happened to the world. She tried floating to see more.

Her feet wouldn't lift off the ground. She stumbled forward into a startling glitch and coughed up dark matter. It was the essence that made up Deities. Only when you exerted yourself would it come up like vomit in a dying patient.

Her mind was spinning. Her powers were gone. She wasn't healed. She couldn't feel where Shào or the Others were in the world.

Weak.

She ran. None of that mattered right now. All that did matter was that Hassan and Hadiya were alive and close.

It was early morning. This must've been a crossbreed-designated city—all she saw were the half-human, half-animal people. They were going to work and starting school in ugly uniforms. All their canals were either dried up or had an inch of frothy water in them: a lawless, dirty city.

The strings brought her down a street of graffiti and palm trees. On the road were more bicycles than cars. The strings, dangling on telephone wires, led to a three-story apartment building atop a clothing store.

Upstairs, in the tightest corner of the room, a light was on.

Mind blank, Maïmoú tried for the front door. Her hand went straight through the handle as if she were all but a phantom to the world. She, dazed, opted to walk straight through it into a living room.

An osprey woman was filling up a bowl of water from the kitchen sink. Once done, she grabbed spare rags and hurried them up the stairs. Maïmoú followed. This house, it smelled like them.

There was a commotion coming from the lit bedroom. Streamers and balloons were attached throughout the hall for some type of celebration. Maïmoú liked to think it was for her and this very special moment.

The woman entered the room, leaving the door partly ajar for Maïmoú to squeeze through.

An orange monkey popped a party popper over the bed. It rained down on a new mother and father, each one cradling a newborn in the softest blanket.

Maïmoú stood in the doorway, eyes affixed to the two babies. She held where her heart was and followed the two strings of fate that, once untangled, led to each child's own heart. She felt their heartbeats beat with hers as if her own ears were pressed up to their chests.

Her knees gave out. She fell to the floor as this new family congratulated the birth of Maïmoú's reincarnated mother and father.

She wept. Out of happiness, anger, delight, and fear, she cried for her parents being reborn to a strange, confusing world where she was incapacitated for a reason that wasn't her fault.

And she smiled from ear to ear, so hard that it hurt, at this new lease on life.

―――◇◇◇―――

That night, after fighting to be physical in this cruel world and failing, Maïmoú nestled within the babies' crib. Her body hardly fit, her back pressing against the wooden beams, but she was able to cradle the two. They were so soft and pink. Their wings hadn't yet grown feathers. They breathed in tandem with each other like they rehearsed it.

She touched the closest one's cheek, held the farthest one's hand. She felt their warmth like the summer Sun. She'd heard that their parents decided on the names Derek and Kevin. She'd never heard two more perfect names.

"Don't worry," she whispered to them. "I'll protect you this time. This time, you'll live long, great lives, and we'll be together." She kissed each of their foreheads. "Forever."

She didn't sleep that night, nor any other night for the next twenty years, to keep that promise.

THE AFFINITY BETWEEN US
Epilogue

The family of Derek, Kevin, and Nikki was quite a lawless one. It was complex, a mixture of model citizens and revolutionaries, all of whom, despite their type A and B personalities, would always find their way back to one another, cities and worlds be damned.

Days after the crossbreeds and the humans reconnected in England—it will soon be known as the Convergence—people began asking questions. It was what they did. As curious as they were afraid, humans and crossbreeds questioned the purpose of one other in fervor. Debates turned to reconciliation which turned to outcry which turned to violence. Fights broke out across the kingdom as food and protection became pressing issues.

Half of the new world's population was now without beds. Waterborne in need of water were given the frigid ocean as their only source of oxygen. Frightened birds flew to the mountains and got lost in the endless forests. Parents went days without hearing from their children, some of whom never found each other again. Knights from the Drailian Castle had established minimal help for those in need.

But they would be alright, except the ones who wouldn't be. Those aforementioned fights had gotten deadly, especially in the farmlands far away from the castle. Many landowners didn't appreciate new striped and spotted faces trespassing on their land. None of our main cast had gotten into such fights, although Morgan Owens, owner of the once notorious Morgan's Delicate Sweets and Treats, was the conductor of the rowdiest banters.

Derek, Kevin, and Nikki had found themselves apart from these social upheavals. Derek because he wasn't playing peacekeeper with humans or crossbreeds any longer. Kevin because he wasn't strong enough, neither in voice nor in heart. Nikki had wanted to, thought up ways to distribute resources to those in need, but she'd fallen back to her siblings' sides. She'd just gotten them back, and it wasn't the right time for her to overturn kingdoms. Not yet.

Derek, Kevin, and Nikki, being Derek, Kevin, and Nikki, stayed cooped up inside the castle for the following month. Partly due to the royal heirs' connection to Derek, partly due to Derek, three bottles of vodka in, had alluded to the fact that *he* had done this to punish humankind. Hundreds of thousands of half-animal people scattered across the humans' fields, Barrier broken? Who else could have done it other than Derek Harrow? The humans had tried blaming the demons—dragons—but Derek had made it clear that all of this happened because of him.

And the humans weren't fools. Something about Derek and his family was connected to this new era. It was a conclusion that wasn't far off from the truth.

Without much more to go on, the king and queen had given in and allowed the three special siblings temporary stay. They'd assumed their parents would accompany them, and they had more than enough bedrooms for their stays.

What they hadn't expected were their extended families. Morgan was vastly fascinated by their lifestyles. She'd been given her own personal knight who kept her from unlocking locked doors. She spent a lot of time with the castle historian, Runa. They kept one another from causing knowing mischief behind the Royal's backs.

Derek, Kevin, and Nikki had tried explaining themselves to everyone who asked. How challenging it proved to be, talking about invisible forces. They'd tried speaking to Holly's, Marcos', and Zantl's perspectives, but it hadn't gotten them far. Zantl had become overwhelmed by their questions and locked themselves away in the castle's tallest tower, refusing counsel. Humans and crossbreeds alike feared Marcos and gave him few chances to speak. Holly, she'd gone mute again. Her scribblings could only entertain the royal family for so long. And little Alexi was just that, little. Nobody could speak for her.

And do not worry, lovers of love. Our love interests of our dear friends had reunited within hours of the Convergence. Found everywhere between the Temno Forest to the vacant farmlands. Derek was with Oliver from the get-go. Nikki had gone out searching for Tokala the second she had her family members accounted for. Kevin, he had more difficulty locating his mudskipper lover. She and Tokala had been separated and therefore had trouble finding their way in the world. Before Kevin's mind told him that she was dead in a world he knew little about, he'd found Viper lost in a nearby town. He had no power to fly—his wing was still broken—but luckily Derek and his levitating, draconic friends knew the area well.

After introductions were said and done and kisses were given aplenty, the skies had cleared, metaphorically and physically. The Barrier around the country had cracked. It was a total upheaval, and those who could take charge did. They explored, learned more, gave these newcomers a chance.

Derek, Kevin, and Nikki did their best to interpret everyone's needs, but as they did, as they made sure no one else on this Earth died, their bodies gave up. They found themselves slogging, sleeping the whole day away and still yawning at breakfast. You'd find them asleep on the same couch, entangling their strings of fate. After withstanding the immense love of Deities in a short amount of time, their bodies had turned to pudding, and they'd found few ways of making their bodies work, other than the love of their family and friends.

After a late night with Oliver in the comforts of the castle, Derek did what he'd never done in all of his recollected memories: He'd woken up early.

The castle was being treated more and more like a hotel you'd find in a high-class society. People came in and out in search of something, whether it be favors or demands or hearings for such favors and demands to be heard. Derek saw waterborne, cats, dogs, and deer walking alongside human knights and farmers. It was early enough today that he only saw maids, but give it a few more hours and the castle would be crawling with beings.

Leaving Oliver a mess in bed, Derek made his way up a spiral stairwell wearing a cloak. Very mysterious, but it was the best way to keep warm. It'd just turned January and snow was piling up outside. Ice frosted over the windows. The ocean was bluer than ever before, especially up so high.

"Shit, shit, shit," he muttered up the stairs. A cloak, he did bring. Shoes fashionable for winter weather, he did not. He nearly flew up the remaining flight in order to gain access to the top floor.

He pushed the top door open with his bottom. "Why the *fuck* did we choose this meeting place?"

Feathers rustled behind him. "Because it's the prettiest view."

Derek went to swing his wing before Kevin blocked it with his good one. His broken wing had been healing nicely, but it'd take a few more months before he could fly again.

"I know you like it up here, Kev," Derek said, "but it's fucking cold. Why not a meeting by the fireplace, or underground in the dungeons?"

"I am *not* going back underground after the year I lived through, Derek. Forget about that."

"Well, *I* want to get through winter without getting sick. All these council meetings are so shitty to listen to. I have a constant headache pretending to listen to them."

"Join the club." Kevin walked down the hall that would lead them to their destination. "Did we make a decision yet?"

"I've been asked that a thousand times this week. Shorten the list."

"The decision between us three."

"On who had the shittiest year?" Derek clarified. "I almost died, like, four times."

"Yeah, but remember when I told you about my elevator crash? And me breaking my wing?"

"I got choked out by Shào."

"Nikki got choked by Maïmoú. She got you beat."

"Okay, but I fucked the most incredible guy who will always be in love with me."

"*That* made your year shitty?"

Derek grinned as they reached the final door. The handle was frigid to the touch. "No. Just wanted to rub it in your face that you're still a *virgin*."

Kevin slapped him with his bad wing, causing him to topple over and Derek to laugh in his face.

The door opened to the west-facing side of the castle rooftop. It was where the king kept his carrier pigeons and hawks during the summer. Now, all the little doors were swinging open on the ocean breezes.

Nikki was sitting in-between the castle merlons, one leg dangling as she looked over the ocean. She had a quill in one hand while the other kept the scarf over her lips. Her face had gone pink from her stay outside.

When the door opened, her rat ears pricked. "We agreed on seven this morning, yeah?"

"Isn't it seven now?" Derek asked.

Nikki held out her thumb above the horizon waves and measured their distance to the Sun. "It's seven thirty, at least."

"There's no way you learned how to do that in mere days of being here."

"You're right. I learned it in hours."

"Derek made me late," Kevin was quick to tattle. "He kept bragging about his sleeping arrangements with that tall fellow."

Derek battled his twin out of the doorway and hopped onto his chosen merlon. "*I* wasn't late. I simply couldn't find my shoes."

"That's not good. Haven't you been here the longest?" Nikki playfully hit him in the knee, then made space for Kevin.

"What're you working on?" Kevin asked her.

Nikki opened up the journal she had bookmarked. "That historian let me borrow her maps."

"Runa," Derek said. "I was wondering if you met her yet."

"There's hundreds of books in the library about nautical navigation, how to read the stars, the sky, how people here lived for generations."

"Anything ringing any bells?" Derek asked. "You were human once, right?"

"You were, too. And Kev."

"Yes, but you seem to remember a lot more than Derek and I can dig up," Kevin said. "I think it's because there's less of a gap between you and him than us and our reincarnations."

"That's another thing I don't get," Derek said. "Were you and I married, Kev? Were we living together, raising that girl together?"

"I told you, she's not just a mere girl."

"Yeah, but I haven't even officially met her yet. While you were off being dragged into elevators by her weird mind powers, I was getting choked out and tossed around by Shào."

"Sorry, again, for that," Nikki said, but Derek waved her off.

"You're not responsible for him. But were we with Maïmoú?"

"I don't think we were married," Kevin said, "whatever that term means here."

"Like Mom and Dad, and how Morgan and Del are. Partners."

"Right. I don't think we were that. I think we were just caring for her."

"I'd trade what you had with Maïmoú with what I have with Shào any day," Nikki said. "It sucks."

"Oh, about our competition," Derek said. "I'm still saying it's me. I talked with three, no, *four* Deities, I think, and they all tried to drown me."

"I got body-snatched and destroyed half the city," Nikki said casually, "and got shot. And Kev was around Maïmoú almost every single day."

"Looks like she had a favorite parent way back when," Derek said. "She must be a daddy's girl."

Kevin looked to the morning sky. "You two still haven't heard from them?"

Nikki took her quill and mapped something in the ocean with one squint eye. "Not a peep."

"Nothin'," Derek said. "And I don't think the others have either. Holly and stuff."

"It's like they disconnected from us."

"Deities disconnecting from the world sounds good," Derek said. "Hate that for us."

"Yeah," Nikki said. "All this wouldn't have happened if Maïmoú hadn't interfered."

"If she hadn't, we'd all be underwater," Kevin reminded her.

"But we wouldn't have been underwater if the Barreira hadn't been placed around her in the first place," Derek countered. "Wait, am I supposed to defend her? She's *my* Deity, right?"

"She—" Nikki stopped herself and took a breath. "Stop it. We promised each other. No talks of Deities like this. We'll deal with them when...*if* they show up again. Right now, we set our sights on what's ahead of us."

Today was all shades of blue, from the darkest waters of the ocean to the brilliant shine of the Sun. Birds cawed above the water, some animals, some crossbreed. The three siblings watched for familiar faces.

"It's pretty here," Nikki said.

"It is," Kevin agreed.

"I suppose," Derek said. "What're we going to do next?"

"I want to help people find homes and a community here," Nikki said. "They can't all keep wandering about like refugees. They'll need a place to call their own."

"Are you going to build houses for them?" Derek asked.

"Maybe. I've already told this to the queen and that little Zantl."

"Little—Jabel?" Derek laughed. "Nikki, he and Zantl are not the same."

"Still learning. Anyway, they seem reasonable. The kids, not the parents. I'll make things work."

"I'd like to make a home for the waterborne," Kevin said. "There're a lot of children in need of help. They have those hot springs scattered through the forest, but those in need of saltwater can't get their water from the ocean. It's too cold."

"I bet your little *friend* can help with that," Derek teased. "What was her name again?"

"*Stop*." Kevin went to hit him again. Despite just getting him back, Kevin and Nikki were ready to hit Derek when they thought he deserved it.

"Like you're so above bringing up someone's lover as a joke?" Derek countered.

"I don't parade my love life around like you do. We're still... talking. It's complicated, wanting to ask out a girl during all...this."

Nikki went to agree, then went red-faced and changed the subject. "You've known Oliver for a few months now, haven't you? That's pretty serious, given your track record."

"Suppose so," Derek said. "He's nice."

"You said his love is like a Deity's love, that you're his mate. That he'll only ever love you."

"Yeah."

"Then you should marry him."

Derek's wings fluffed up. "I-it's not that easy here."

"But don't humans get married to their loved ones?"

"It's way more complicated than that. Let's, uh, talk about something else."

"Ooh, struck a nerve?" Nikki poked Derek with the blunt side of her quill. "The thought of commitment turned you off?"

It was the exact opposite, but Derek played it off as if marriage wasn't in the cards for him. "Anyway. Who won? Who had the shittiest year?"

They all pretended to think about it, letting the sky swirl with colors of a brighter future.

"I don't know who's the winner or loser," Nikki said, "but I know that I'm the happiest I've ever been in a long time. So, I win," she added. Her tail was wagging as she spoke, betraying her nonchalant wording.

"Aw," Derek cooed, "how cute. That means you *love* us, don't you? You *love* us."

"I did not risk my life and fight for you two every day if I didn't. You two are my everything. Don't forget it."

Kevin hugged her waist and pulled her in closer. Derek, jealous, snatched her up and played tug of war with her middle.

"Gonna throw up," Nikki warned them. "I'm serious, I will throw up on you both and I won't feel sorry about it!"

"Then we'll have to throw you over the edge!" Derek leaned her too far back and made her squeak.

"Too soon!" Kevin yelled, and pulled all three of them back. Feathers flew up in a flurry of white. The three of them collapsed onto each other, laughing together, their hearts now one.

THE BONDS WE SHARE
Prologue

---◆ ☾ ◆---

Alliroue Amir, age sixteen, had been working on a naked boy's body for most of her adolescent life.

Technically, he was a humanoid, a robot constructed of wires and natural polymers, and he still didn't have a face. It was currently set aside on her rolling workstation beside a half-finished bag of potato chips and a blunt.

Sticking the blunt back in her mouth, Alliroue focused on Marcos' arm. There were two wires that kept entangling themselves inside his forearm. They couldn't seem to separate no matter what Alliroue did, and if she sealed it away and pretended it wasn't a big deal, they'd burn through his artificial skin and kill him.

Not that he was alive—not yet. August fourth was the date she'd set for herself, the date she'd officially turn Marco Amir on and let him loose in the world that was currently on fire.

Maybe it was selfish, creating a robot during a pandemic, wasting time tinkering when she could've been helping those suffering from the radiation sickness that was IRE-21, but this was her passion project. For longer than she'd been a teenager, she'd been painstakingly focused on creating this one-of-a-kind model through patents and grants the country had so generously gifted her. It'd been on the news, her work, alongside her as a person. Ever since she was a toddler and the Deity of Earth had accepted her as his newly adopted daughter, she'd been in that burning spotlight.

She shivered in ninety-degree weather. She focused on her boy. That was all she could do. With her lofi music on high and AC turned off, Alliroue hyperfixated on his brain's programming.

The hours slipped by, the best kind of therapy. The work that not only made her happy but fulfilled, like she deserved to live and work on things to make the world slightly better. The world was arguably worse on days she thought she was good enough to live, but sometimes, she had to power through to make her children.

One of them approached her, reminding her that she hadn't eaten anything in over twelve hours. Her little Sauria, the dinosaur-shaped robots she'd designed in a fugue state and just kept making more of because it was fun. Dozens of them waddled around in her apartment. They helped her with cleaning.

"Alright, alright." She scratched the underneath of its chin, eliciting a calming purr from it as its cheeks pinkened. "I'm getting up."

She cracked her joints one by one as she beelined for her kitchen. Groceries arrived at her door by servbots daily, but she seldom used them. With only herself living here—not including her several hundred plants breathing life into her stuffy rooms—she didn't exactly know how to feed herself real meals. Her best was a bowl of cereal with almond milk only two days expired.

Her phone pinged in the upper-hand corner of her vision. A light flashed, alerting her to an instant message. She opened it up with her mind.

Lí bby *9:09*
hey allibop you awake yet?

Alliroue burst into an uncontainable grin. She responded back with fluttering eyelashes and a thumping heart. Their last text message was over two weeks ago, of him asking her about Marcos' progress and her mental health.

Me *9:09*
Yeah! How are you? Are you in Pangea?

Lí bby *9:10*
I'm downstairs. I heard movement.

Gasping, Alliroue stomped her feet. "You asshole!" she shouted. "You piece of shit! Why didn't you tell me you were here?"

Lí bby *9:10*
Is that you upstairs?
Alliroue how old are you www
Stopppppp

Giggling, Alliroue kept jumping until she startled one of her Sauria into the dining room. Lí was here, in Pangea. Not a thousand miles away, not being dragged around the world by Shào, unsure of where he'd be sleeping that night. This was his home, as it was hers, and Salem's.

Dashing into the foyer, Alliroue donned her jean jacket and snatched up her hoverboard sitting upright by the door. Unlocking it with her mind, she then sprinted down to the elevators.

She crashed into a bundle of blankets. She backpedaled, hitting her back into the hallway wall before she tripped any more on the dragging fabric.

"Hello there," the bundle said. "Is the building on fire?"

"*Salem.*" Alliroue shook out the brown and white curls from her face. "You scared me."

Salem bowed a somewhat respectable bow to her. They were wrapped in one of their many blankets, cloaked like a scary villain. That look was tarnished by their sheep slippers and bedhead mess of brown hair surrounding their actual sheep horns. "Am I not allowed to wander?"

"No, but you barely make a sound when you move." She was going to chide them on the dangers of dragging blankets around their slippered feet, especially if they took the stairs, but she held her tongue. It was nice to see them out of their room. Lately, they spent more and more time withdrawn, their depression overcoming them into isolation. She understood and let it be. "Lí's back home," she added. "He's downstairs."

They looked between their slippered feet to the floor beneath them. They moved one out of the way as if checking for shit. "I got him presents. Him and Tai."

"Ooh, I wonder if he brought him along?"

"Probably. The two are hardly ever separate."

Alliroue followed Salem down the elevator into their place, hoping they wouldn't bump into Lí between floors. Luckily, they were safe, save for a few servbots spotcleaning the windows.

"What present did you get him?" Alliroue asked. "It's been forever since we saw him."

Salem unlocked their door. "Nothing big. You know how he hates grand gestures."

Alliroue, nosy about her friends' lives, snuck a peek into a place she seldom entered.

It was like a cave: curtains drawn, all the fluorescent lights replaced with dull, orange sensory lighting. Moons and stars glowed along the walls and up the stairwell, and a few of Alliroue's Sauria were tottering along, picking up old plates and socks. Salem had loved space ever since they were the prime minister's child in England. Now, after denouncing their father, country, and most of civilization, Alliroue wondered if they preferred it simply because it meant being as far away from beings as possible.

Maybe that's why they'd booked a flight to the Moon next summer. Smarter than most law students, Salem had recently been accepted to be a part of the European lunar base space project. A community of people living on the Moon, aiming to further the progress of beingkind.

That, or it was the only place in the actual known universe where Deities couldn't bother them.

Salem came back with a package pre-wrapped by skilled hands.

"What's that?"

"A mouse doll. The seller said it helps calm you down if you squish your face against it. I've been waiting to give it to him in person."

"Aw, I'm sure he'll love it. But you're showing me up, aren't you? I should've planned to give him something, too. All I do is send him care packages and hope he's in whatever town long enough to receive them."

"Well, you did better than I've done in the past year. This's all I got him."

"Aw, I didn't mean it that way. Come on, let's go find him before he runs off to another country."

"Off to help the world while we suffocate ourselves."

"Suffocate ourselves? Open a window, Salem. It's nice out."

They stuck out their tongue.

The elevator down the hall beeped, and a pair of quiet footsteps walked out to greet them.

"Hey," Lí said, greeting them with a gentle wave. "You talking about me, yeah?"

"Lí!" Alliroue dashed down the hall, arms wide to grab him first. He still smelled like himself, like dark coffee and life outside. He was still short, still warm, still alive. His stubble was unkempt and he needed a good brush. She squeezed him as if he'd slip through her arms if she wasn't careful enough.

"Oh, wow." Another person came out of the elevator, towering over all of them. Bright, bleach-white hair with a tinge of pink in his bangs, Tai welcomed himself by scooping both Lí and Alliroue up in two arms. "No hi for me? I'm the one who forced him to come by for a week."

"A *week*? You're here for a *week*?" Alliroue couldn't control herself and kissed Tai on the cheek. He was the newest addition to their small circle of friends, but with his mannerisms and calming attitude, Alliroue had welcomed Lí's fiancé wholly. "You work magic on him, Tai. I've been begging him to come for months!"

"I was busy in Europe!" Lí said.

At the European namedrop, Salem pretended to barf all over their blanket. Alliroue laughed as Tai rustled her hair.

Lí managed a smile. "Anyway, you're good, yeah? Allibop? Salem?"

While Salem merely shrugged, Alliroue lied and said, "I'm better now that you're here."

"I'm good as I can be," Salem added, and grabbed Lí's hand in a forceful handshake two brothers would share.

Their banter brought a smile to each of their sleepy faces, and Alliroue couldn't contain herself and hugged them together, a first in what felt like billions of years.

"How'd you get him to stay here?" Alliroue asked Tai.

"You could see it in his eyes. He needed to come home, albeit for a second."

"How is he?"

Shrugging away a verbal response, he instead went over to his lover and hugged him. Physical touch had never been one of his love languages, but since meeting his other half, he'd been more welcoming to it.

She dragged three of her closest friends back to her place, their preferred place of hanging out due to Salem living like a cave crab and Lí literally having only *a* bed and *a* couch and nothing else—living like an actual homeless person even though he had the power and money to buy an island. Tai had a home in Australia where he and Lí had first met, but ever since IRE-21 charred most of the country, they were more "fly-by-the-seat-of-their-pants" nowadays, grabbing hotels nearest their place of work.

Pretending she was a good host, Alliroue offered them their drinks of choice: Lí got iced mocha, Salem got a raspberry sprite that tasted more like battery acid than a drink, and Tai got hot milk like an insane person.

They caught up slowly, mostly with Lí and Tai and his travels around the world. He told them how his proposal went even though they'd gone over it dozens of times on FaceTime. They couldn't dive heavily into the topic of their work—nobody wanted to be reminded of the destruction of a dying world—but they tiptoed around it, allowing any of them to talk about it if they needed to.

They didn't, and instead kept bringing the conversation back to Alliroue, much to Alliroue's dismay.

"How's he coming along?" Lí asked, finishing his second cup of coffee that hour. "Is he decent? I'd love to see him."

"Currently, he doesn't have a face. I had to take it off and tweak his orbital receptor because it keeps giving me problems."

"I feel like every time we hear from you, something else goes wrong with him," Salem said as they bundled themselves deeper in their blanket. "You should just turn him on and see what happens."

"You *have* been working on him for ages," Lí said. "Not to undermine you—"

"To severely undermine you," Tai translated.

Lí pushed him farther away on the couch. "But aren't you nitpicking him at this point?"

"I don't think so," she said, knowingly lying again. As a creative, she knew that perfection wasn't possible, not when it came to robotics. That was what updates were for, that's why she had extra parts to fix him if and when he ever turned on. She *had* turned him on, once, for real, but she'd overheated him by keeping him on the charger and he'd powered down on top of her before opening his eyes. And having a stiff, 200-pound robot fall on top of you and being too embarrassed to call someone to help, she'd resulted in asking Tsvetan to come save her.

The embarrassment of that failure and having her adoptive father come rescue her kept her from being so brazen again. In all honesty, he was likely ready to be fully functional, able to experience this hateful world like a newborn. But knowing it'd lead to her being in the news again...

She rolled on her hips, biting her lower lip.

"You don't have to show us if you don't want to," Lí said. "It's just a thought."

"I'm pressuring her," Salem said. "Fuck it. It's not like you won't learn anything by turning him on. Plus, I want to meet him."

"I do, too," Tai said. "All I've heard from Lí here is that you're making this one-of-a-kind, totally amazing, incredible, sexy—"

"Excuse me," Lí said. "I did not say that."

"He is, though, ain't he?"

"Do not talk about my son like that in front of me," Alliroue said, but she started getting up regardless, stretching to give herself more time. "I...suppose I can turn him on. Once. For us."

"Really?" Salem asked. "Shit. I didn't think you'd actually do it."

"Peer pressure wins!" Tai jumped to his feet to help Lí up on his old-man knees. "Let's go. Where is he? In your room?"

"He's in my lab—wait, wait! Don't go in just yet."

"Oh, you got porn pulled up on every computer screen?"

"Ew, no!" she said, but she actually didn't know if she'd exited out of the recent hentai she'd been perusing that morning.

"Oo, Alliroue got lesbian porn up!" Tai called out through the penthouse, and ran for her lab. Alliroue, red-faced and laughing, chased after them, they who thought it was funny to laugh along to her humiliation.

She beat all three doofuses to her lab, where Marcos was still sitting faceless on the workstation. Her little Sauria had done an excellent job cleaning up the space since she'd left, leaving neither a crumb nor bolt on the floor. She petted each of their bobbing heads for a job well done.

She wiped her hands on her jean shorts, sweat coating her palms as she faced Marcos. She'd expected an audience for his turning on, but having that audience be her closest friends was nerve-wracking. Their opinions mattered most to her, affecting her more so than whatever tabloid lied about her.

"He looks incredible," Lí said.

"He's like a supermodel," Salem added.

"Does he have super powers?" Tai asked. "Can he shoot fire like a dragon?"

"Oh, please," Alliroue said, though she did have the blueprints for it.

Hesitantly, she crept up to Marcos. He was beautiful: soft, blond hair, with crystal blue eyes and fair skin without a blemish to be seen—she wasn't stupid enough to make a robot not attractive. By all means, he looked much too cool to be friends with her. And she hadn't programmed his emotions to be unconditional. What if he hated her? What if he thought her interests were boring and decided to leave her? He could go off on missions like Lí, or travel to the Moon with Salem. Maybe he'd come to despise her like so many others online. Maybe...

Maybe he'd be her best friend. It was just like Salem had said, she wouldn't know unless she tried.

"Back up, then," Lí said, keeping Tai back like an excited puppy. "Give her some space."

"Do you need help?" Salem asked, scooting back a touch. "I can whack him on."

"No whacking." Alliroue disconnected him from the battery charger so he didn't overheat again. His processors were on, his receptors seemed good. He was clothed, too, wearing a pair of jeans she kept him in to keep his dignity. Everything seemed okay, okay as a quiet morning with the chance of everything going to Hell.

"Oh, shoot." She quickly reattached his face, clicking it into place behind his ears, against his scalp, underneath his chin. She held up her hands, waiting to see smoke billow out of his ears.

Two floating screens came up around her, warning her that the Marcos Unit was being turned on.

20%.

55%.

70%.

Every inch the green meter grew, the sicker Alliroue felt. There was a slim chance nothing went wrong and she'd be the mother of the world's most efficient humanoid. She held her breath, hoping for the best but expecting the absolute worst.

A familiar pop of energy burst next to her, shocking her off her unsteady feet. She almost half-expected it to be a machine exploding in flames, but she knew that sound. All of them did, unfortunately or not.

Tsvetan, Deity of the Earth, appeared in Alliroue's lab. He was floating due to his absent left leg and divine abilities, and looked out of breath. It looked like he'd run to get here and, for a moment, didn't know where he was or what he teleported into.

Lí grabbed hold of Tai's hand, fear striking his heart at who that could've been. Poor Tai, unable to see divinity, had to pick up on their body clues and where their eyes were looking. Salem looked up, not for Tsvetan, but for their own Deity, Unathi, to appear.

"What's going on?" Alliroue asked her Deity. She saw Tsvetan like a dad, somewhat, but he had this strange aura to him, reminding her that he wasn't entirely human. And a Deity appearing without notice was never a good sign, dad-like or not.

"I...don't know," Tsvetan said. "The energy here, it's..." He doubletook the room, frightening Salem back a full step. Mushrooms bloomed and decayed on his tan skin. "What's going on?"

Another bubble burst near her windows. "What the fuck is going on?" asked a stern voice.

Alliroue's heart swelled and numbed like a bee sting. Sabah had entered her penthouse without warning, striding into the room with boots cracking the tiles. She was detailing the room like a police officer scanning a suspicious room, lip curled in disgust.

"I-is something wrong?" Alliroue asked, now fearing for her own life. Tsvetan coming here wasn't that out of the ordinary, but Sabah was a gift, or a curse. Alliroue never visited Earth without a just cause.

Salem found the nearest door and was ready to sprint back to their safe haven that was their dark room. Tsvetan and Sabah were one thing, but if Unathi came, that was it. Salem would relapse, Lí would fight for their honor and safety from a predator who'd hurt them beyond repair. Alliroue would…

Spiral. This was supposed to be a get-together with close friends. Tsvetan and Sabah, while sometimes nice to be around together, would always end disastrously. The thought of even inviting them to this event hadn't even crossed her mind—she just wanted one moment with her friends.

Marcos' computers dinged. His body booted up and automatically straightened his spine. His fingers cracked and made fists by his thighs. His mouth twitched.

Tsvetan's and Sabah's attention pulled to his turning on. They watched the machines they didn't understand and the screens they couldn't comprehend tell them his status as a newly-made being. They watched as his eyes slowly opened under his wave of sunshine blond hair. He lifted his head to them, taking them in, taking in divinity.

Tsvetan covered his mouth with one hand, eyes widening in shock. Lí watched him, then looked to Alliroue to discern what was happening. Alliroue watched Marcos move for the first time, a child taking their first steps. He looked fine. His vitals were normal in her robotic vision.

What wasn't normal, and what she hadn't expected, was the way he was looking directly at two beings he shouldn't have been able to see. His head cocked to each of them, and then he kept his processing eyes on Sabah.

Sabah, Deity of all water, filled with hatred for everything beings stood for, slumped at being perceived. Her shoulders fell, face blank as they shared a moment of clarity.

Tsvetan wrapped a trembling hand over Sabah's. "What... is this?"

"What's what?" Alliroue asked, but the answer was coming to her regardless of the probability. She had no memories of the time she'd first met Tsvetan, but he'd explained it quite similarly to what Sabah was looking like: the trajectory of your life, all your morals and beliefs, being altered the second you met someone who filled your heart with such unbridled love—soulmates, the beings able to see Deities.

Sabah, unable to come to terms with what'd just happened to her, turned and broke eye contact with Marcos. Then she glanced back, started walking towards nowhere specific, then turned back again to make sure he was there.

Marcos cocked his head, his eyes dilating on her figure.

Sabah shivered and broke away yet again. "H-how did you do this?" she asked the room, out of breath even though she'd only taken a few steps. "How did you make a soulmate?"

"I-I don't know," Alliroue answered. "I just...*made* him. Did you...?"

"How is this possible?" Tsvetan interrupted. "I didn't know you could...*None* of us...He's a robot."

"Robots...can have souls," Lí said. "They're capable, yeah?"

"But this can't be happening." At a loss for words, Tsvetan retook Sabah's hand and pet it. She became frozen as an ice sculpture as her world—and Earth itself—had been changed.

Alliroue licked her lips to apologize or find a new explanation for what she'd just created. Another soulmate connected to a Deity, from her own hands, unknowingly. If she knew this would've happened, she would've burned Marcos' blueprints years ago. To be tied to a Deity, like them...

It was a death sentence.

Sabah wiped her arms of something gross. "Keep him away from me," she muttered.

"Sabah—"

"No!" she shouted at Tsvetan, jumping the room. "I am not to be within a mile of that thing. Keep him—all of you..."

Cursing him in Old World Speak, Sabah vanished as quickly as she'd come, leaving all of their lives forever altered by Alliroue's creation.

THE BONDS WE SHARE
Epilogue

———————— ◆ ☾ ◆ ————————

Holly disliked most activities when not in Oliver's company.

This world, so strange and vast and always changing, often overwhelmed her. Carriages? Horses? Knights and castles with crowns passing to similar-shaped heads? She'd seen the process roll over many times, attending coronations through bushes or underneath evergreen pine.

Some things made sense, like the ebbing tides and changing seasons. She understood why the world switched clothes, despite her fear of it. But sometimes, it became too much to bear. Simple outings for food became tasks too daunting to complete, and she had to stay in bed for many days to process it all. Roads were being paved right before her eyes. Little babies she saw in the markets were suddenly having babies of their own.

To battle these present fears, she took her walks. In the middle of the night, when field mice and owls called to each other in the forest. When the Moon was at its brightest and dawning to meet its lover, she enjoyed living, then. She was able to breathe safely in the safety of the trees.

When she planned trips without warning, the demons of the manor got fussy. Yomi would pause her knitting and watch her leave from the couch, and Shimah would quiz her.

"Where're you going?"

"You sure you packed everything?"

"D'ya really know how to get back here by yourself?"

Most people acted this way around her, even humans, when they weren't throwing stones at her or calling her miserable names. She was a worrisome girl who worried others, and no amount of preparation she did for her journeys would sway their feelings.

She did always try, though. She, despite her abilities, never wanted to make anyone nervous.

That was challenging with Oliver. He was in the kitchen that morning, washing out a mug in the sink to be used for his morning tea. Shimah had started a fire in the fireplace, where they'd warm up nice hot cups for everyone in the house. She, like Oliver, liked a cup of herbal tea to start her morning.

"Good morning, Holly," said Oliver. "You're up early."

Holly skipped the last three steps of the stairs. She almost tripped and landed on her ankle wrong, but through fate or some other benign spirit, she made it to the first floor unscathed. It happened often, her defying physics. The demons stopped questioning it. Holly never had.

They all knew she rarely spoke, but Oliver was the most patient with her. A few words escaped every now and then, but she often kept mute for her own sanity. To help, she pulled out one of her babies. Dollies, stuffies, little toys sewn with hay, grass, and old pieces of fabric. She had several dozen in her room and hidden away in nooks and crannies of the manor. Today, she had a little girl in a dress and button eyes. Holly made her dolly nod for her.

Oliver nodded back and showed her her seat and cup. "I was just about to go outside for a run after I did these dishes. Would you like to join me?"

Holly climbed onto her chair and sniffed the cup before drinking it. She was planning a morning out by herself, but having Oliver offer first was nice. She nodded her dolly and enjoyed her tea in one long sip.

"Good. Are you alright today?"

She thought about it. Her brain was normally a jar of bees too shaken to fly straight, a buzzing cacophony. Today, the bees were still asleep, silently vibrating against one another for warmth. She nodded her dolly just once.

Oliver continued washing his mug, watching her out of the corner of his eyes. "Are you sure you're okay? Your tail is thumping."

Was it? She didn't know. She had no idea how to check in with her brain or heart—if she became too buzzy, she just ran. Ran away mentally or physically, into caves or into the depths of the forest for days on end.

She listened for any buzzing. Other than a twitch in her ears, everything seemed fine to her. Another nod. Another for good measure.

Oliver chuckled and poured himself a cup of tea. "You're so funny, Hollybean."

A prickle went down her spine, and she smiled into her steaming cup. If her tail wasn't thumping now, it sure was with that nickname. Nicknames confused her, but that one made her smile.

It was her favorite time outside: dawn. Before the lovers danced in the sky, when the air was cool and crisp and felt like true air, not just the air around you. The birds were waking with the world. They chirped from branches, hip-hopping around the pine. Their path wound around the prettiest parts of the forest and kept her attention for over ten minutes. It was autumn, her favorite season: hot, but not enough to lose her sweaters; beautiful morning skies; the flowers. Living so far away from society allowed them to bloom and blossom without fear of fires or roads. The quietness of forests, she enjoyed it almost as much as her dollies.

Placing her dolly atop her head, she freed up her hands and wrapped her arms around Oliver. One of her limp hands interlaced with his, keeping her even closer to her very good friend.

Oliver leaned more of his weight against hers. He hummed with the birds' songs. She almost dozed off to the melody as he became her musical guide.

"Ow!"

She opened her eyes and instantly looked down at her feet, checking for any pitfalls or thorns. Around the bend, yes, but nothing in front of them.

Oliver wrenched his arm free from Holly's grip. She'd been unintentionally squeezing him, digging her claws into his arm. "What's wrong, dear?"

She patted her head for her baby and found that her ears were twitching back and forth. Her body was tensing, alert. Her eyes, they were now wide, attention snapping every which way. Her tail, her tiptoes, her nose, frantically sniffing the air.

Oliver gave her space, holding her hand as leverage but not letting go. And thank goodness for that—she was now feeling like the soft winds of the forest were going to blow her away.

Electric energy was building inside her like lightning before thunder. The hairs on the back of her neck were standing on end. Something was wrong, desperately and horribly. Or something was very good? She didn't know, but she felt, at once, getting sick on the forest floor or bursting into tears in laughter.

And so, like always, like how she lived, she ran. Tucking her dolly into her bosoms, she bolted into the thicket. With the maps of the forest burned inside her brain, she dodged boulders, hopped over fallen logs, and skipped over streams to...

Her ears twitched again and again, this way and that. Something was upsetting her brain. She was missing a piece of it and it wouldn't stop buzzing until she found the piece. But what was happening? What was she thinking, or feeling?

He's here.

That voice. She heard many voices in her head, some of which weren't her own. She learned early on in life that some people heard voices, but not like hers. Hers sounded like someone was whispering against the tiny hairs in her ears. They were rare—she swore she heard those voices more often in the early years of her life—but now...

He's on the beach, if you wish to see him. I brought him here, just for you.

A boy, or a person with a soft voice, like Oliver but different. Distant, sad.

Comforting. Incredibly heartwarming, like a fond memory once lost.

I entrust him with you, the Little Voice said. *You, who know the tribulations of this life. Take care of him, as I know you'll do well.*

She continued running, this time with a destination in mind, all the while overthinking this man's voice and who he was to her. Had she heard him before? When she dreamed, did she dream of this man? She heard Oliver calling for her, but this voice was even closer, like he was floating right beside her as she ran.

Tossing all that aside, she continued on until she broke through to the smell of salt.

She scrunched her nose as she overlooked the end of the world. She'd climbed up a hill to overlook the cliffs of the sea. Another hop or skip and she would've plunged to her death, or a rather fast fall, wherein she would magically be saved, just like always, by magical, caring hands.

She allowed herself one inhale and exhale before assessing her position. To her right was more forest, curving behind her and down the hill. To her left was more ocean but also the beginning of a sandy beach. It stretched south, all the way to the Drailian Castle.

She looked down the white-faced cliffs. The ocean was lapping against the pointed rocks below, begging her to jump. Instead of jumping, she scaled the rocks, choosing her footfalls just right.

"Holly!"

Her foot slipped on a particularly wet stone. Usually, she was a master of scaling large and somewhat questionable structures. But upon hearing her name being called out, unsure if it was Oliver frantically hoping she wouldn't be submerged in the ocean waves, or that man, who she believed would be very handsome and kind.

The wind rushed around her. Her vision flickered. She saw the sky and then the Sun, trying to color the waves in pinks and orange. She shut her eyes at the possibility of death.

But, like always, it didn't happen. Just before she cracked her head on the rocks, her body floated to a stop like she was a demon able to just do that. Some said she was a dragon, but she was just a girl.

Two invisible hands grabbed hold of her armpits and brought her down to the sandy beach. Not by Oliver, not by any being able to fly, but by the voices, those who whispered secrets to her and kept a careful eye on her after all these years.

Just as she floated to her knees, she picked up on this untracked scent. She plodded through the cold sand towards the rising Sun, sniffing the air for whatever she was running towards. She felt like she was on the right track. The electricity was sparking. This "he," this mysterious "him" the Little Voice alluded to, was someone of great importance to her. People like her knew such things: the mentally ill understood fixations, and the stranger and more mundane they were, the better.

I am sorry, said the Little Voice, *for being absent these last few centuries.*

She continued on. She checked behind driftwood, then around a large rock covered in algae.

We've taken a step back from engaging in your life, he continued. *We didn't think our meddling would contribute to a healthy life for you. We'd tried before, but...*

A flock of white and grey seagulls scattered into the sea as she passed them.

We still keep an eye on you, and we'll continue to do so until the end of time. But it won't be like before. Not unless we can help it.

At this point, Holly began ignoring the Little Voice. Which must've been what he wanted, in the end, given what he was monologuing. To her knowledge, she'd never met the man who owned this voice. She was saved, grabbed, pulled away from imminent dangers, but she'd had no justifiable reason for those saves. She surmounted it to God, unfortunately. Unfortunately because, unlike many believers, she'd never once prayed in her life. She didn't think she be granted salvation.

We're sorry, Lea and I. Know that we love you, despite everything. We treasure you, Hollybean.

A stray tear leaked out of one eye. Batting it away, she ran around a cliffside that jutted into the ocean shoreline. Hopping over the wet rocks with care, she broke free to the beach right by the castle.

She breathed out, heaving, and scanned the new horizon line. This beach was much wider, built right against the white cliffs of the Drail Kingdom, and the Sun had risen past the waves. There were a few more seagulls pecking at the wet sand or loafing with their friends, but one bird looked rather distressed.

It looked like it'd landed wrong. One of its wings was pointing at the sky, the other, underneath its poor body. Feathers were scattered around its bruised legs, bobbing in the calming current.

And it wasn't a bird she'd ever seen before. This bird was a boy, or a person, with magnificent bird wings attached to their back. Bird tail, too—part bird, part human.

It took her breath away, her feet drowning in the shoreline waves. He was quite a ways away from her, almost a half mile, but she understood what she was seeing.

A person who was part animal.

A person who was just like her.

"Holly!"

She flinched as two hands grabbed her from behind. Oliver's scent engulfed her as he wheezed from the chase. "What... on Earth...are you running from?"

She shook her head. She wasn't running away from anything. It was what she was running towards, who needed to be saved.

Unable to speak, she pointed Oliver's attention to the unconscious soul on the beach.

After regaining his ability to breathe, he followed her pointed finger. He squinted through the summer glare, even cupping his blackened hand over his forehead to see farther out. He even took a step forward to see what exactly this mound of feathers and ripped clothes was, before understanding what Holly had found and gasping.

"What is that?" he asked, though Holly had no answer for him, to the person on the beach or to why she'd run as far as she'd gone to find him. Something about their aura had attracted her, like bees to honey. If she squinted, she saw red string bundled and twisted around his body, leading out to sea atop the stilling waves. How odd—on certain days, she, too, saw a similar red string, tying her heart to someone far away.

She touched her heart, as did Oliver, as they both admired the person from afar. Oliver, after realizing he was looking at a person, took a step forwards, dipping his boots into the water to better see.

Then he stepped back onto squishy seagrass. He gently took Holly by the arm and brought her around the cliffside, out of danger.

She spotted them seconds after he did. On the opposite side of the beach was a young girl and boy they knew quite well. They must've just left the castle on their private morning strolls: the soon-to-be king and his little sister, Prince Jabel and Princess Cellena Drail.

Holly covered her mouth. They were unattended with no maids or knights protecting them. They shouldn't have been so far away from home, even if theirs was just atop the cliffs.

"W-we need to be out of sight," Oliver warned Holly. "If they spot us, they might think we had something to do with this. C-come now. Back home."

Holly hesitated a second longer. Something had drawn her to the person on the beach, some shared connection that allowed her to find him alone. Was she supposed to help him? Was she meant to find the meaning of his arrival? With wings flecked with white, he might've been an angel sent down by their God. Was it God who was speaking to her just then, in her head?

Surely not, for she didn't think any God had a voice meant to be heard so clearly.

Oliver tugged Holly away, more and more until they were completely hidden behind the shade of the cliffs. Holly fiddled with her sweater ends, as she wanted to go see the boy again. To show this, she nuzzled up against Oliver's side, trying to find his hand to hold.

But he was using both hands to cover his own mouth. Sliding down against the rock, Oliver's knees gave out, and he burst into tears and cried into his blackened hands.

Holly knelt down beside him and rubbed his back. She tried taking a peek at his face to find what had harmed him. Had he stepped wrong and injured his foot? Had a rogue thought derailed his day? She was used to his bouts of fear turning into tears, but this was so sudden.

She stayed with him by the waves, petting him, telling him in her own words that he would be alright. There was a commotion on the other side of the beach—she heard someone speak, a flurry of questions with no clear answers. Oliver, through gasps, dared a peek betwixt the rocks, but it seemed far too great a burden for him. Upon seeing the angel stand, speak, look around this world with bright eyes, he collapsed into another wave of wails. Holly had never seen a man so overcome with grief.

Only when the angel fell back asleep on the coastline, when the royal heirs ran back home seeking help, did Oliver properly take Holly back home.

It was that afternoon, when Oliver was able to speak coherently again, when Holly discovered why Oliver had cried at the sight of the winged person, why he spilled his heart over the craggy rocks of the beach.

After finding out that Oliver's soul had bonded and tied around the nameless angel, after realizing that his tears were not from grief but of happiness, pure, uninhibited gaiety at finding the person who'd complete his heart, did she happily join him in crying.

OUR DIVINE RUIN
Prologue

───────◆ ☾ ◆───────

Fate wasn't wrong about many things in his semi-immortal life, but he *had* been wrong about horses.

He had been close, though. They hadn't become a formidable rival to wolves as beingkind's best friend, now the common household dog, but they played a crucial role to beingkind's progress. Thousands of years of symbiotic relationships and genetic modification and beingkind now housed tiny, wolf-life creatures in their homes. He hadn't expected that. In another near, relative timeline, they would've been horses.

And waterborne had yet to find a way to make lily pads consumable. And the Moon had yet to be struck by an asteroid that'd crack it in two. That one was a childish belief he and his friends had held on to for millions of years. With how many craters peppered its land, it wasn't improbable, and his mind knew it'd happen, as all things would.

But what he *was* certain of, and what he'd known for hundreds of years, was that little Maïmoú of Athens would change the world.

And he did keep hold of the belief about the horses, for Lea's sake. She did love her little horsies. She'd been the one to design them.

Currently, Maïmoú of Athens was going by another name: Selene, her birth name, but she wouldn't be known by that for very long. She'd also change her name for a third time soon, but that was a story for another time. Right now, she was but six years old. Fate couldn't even remember being so small. The trauma spanning millions and millions of years was better left tucked away in the recesses of his mind.

He'd only promised the world a quick visit. He didn't like leaving Lea alone for very long, and coming back to this place did little to lift his spirits. He didn't hate coming back—he loved the world—but knowing what was coming down the pike always upset him.

Still, he had to be here for this. He had to make his presence known, if only to make himself feel better about what was to come.

This morning, he was floating high above Maïmoú of Athen's domicile. Her family owned a modest cottage by the ocean with an acre of land they'd cultivated into a lovely pasture. Chickens and hens clucked through tall, healthy grasses. Wooden toys and stuffed dolls were left abandoned on the side of the home. It smelled wild and carefree, like a certain someone waiting from him in the Void.

Do you see her?

Fate smiled at the voice in his head. "Not yet, my friend," he said aloud. She'd hear him anywhere, even in his thoughts.

I want to see her, Lea said. *She's me, isn't she? Her heart is me. I am her. She's me...*

"She's like you in many ways, yes. She has your spirit. She'll make the perfect substitute, as will he," he added. The "he" in question would be born two hundred years later, but again, another story for another time. "I'll be home soon, my love."

I want to see her.

"I know, my love."

I want to see her.

Fate returned to the cottage. When Lea got like this, when her mind hyper-focused on the outcome and not the work it'd take to get there, it was best to leave her to her thoughts. She couldn't leave the inner workings of his mind, his Void. She was too weak, too damaged by those he'd once called friends. The animal population would only decrease in time, and so when her brain got stuck on a thought, it took her some time to come back to her senses.

He brushed back his long, white hair. He'd been floating here for several minutes, watching from the clouds, wondering if he should simply return to his Void and rest with Lea for another century. He knew he wouldn't, but the hesitance was still there.

He couldn't remember the last time he visited Earth. For his own sanity, he forced himself to forget many of those memories, back when dinosaurs roamed lush rainforests and rain storms washed away continents. Some pain wasn't meant to be relived.

Wiping the sweat from his tattooed palms, Fate descended down to the chimney of Maïmoú's home. It billowed sweetened smoke from a morning breakfast. Loaves of bread dipped in wine with honey—did he smell hints of fig? He was glad to see the little girl was being so well taken care of. In a few years, the people in her life wouldn't be as kind to her as to make sure she was well fed.

Their voices carried through the home. Her mother and father were called Maria and Alexandros. While Fate knew the tragic outcomes of both of their lives, he admired their tenacity to raise such a good daughter. The father was about to leave while the mother would tend to her herb garden and care for her little girl. If only beingkind was as peaceful as this home.

"Selene!"

Fate levitated a few feet higher so his shadow couldn't be seen across the lawn. He didn't want any of their eyes catching his presence. He was just a phantom, a side liner as the world kept turning. It was a role he'd fallen into seamlessly, ever since...

He squeezed his eyes a little tighter, feeling his tattoos swirl with dark matter. Rubbing down his throat, also tattooed—he was tattooed everywhere, by choice and by aesthetic—he kept himself from reminiscing. There was a time and place. He'd be a hypocrite if he started thinking about his friends and how they'd so ruthlessly destroyed kinship and relationships that spanned before the dawn of time.

He breathed in, then out. Maybe he'd cut this visit short. After all, it wasn't like he could speak to the little girl. Her learning about Gods at such an early age wouldn't have been beneficial for anyone. At the end of the day, he was doing this for himself, for the simple, selfish pleasure of dipping his toes into the pond of life and knowing he was still alive. That he could still affect and make change. His Domain was still in the air, sifting the sand in the hourglass. Hourglasses had yet to be invented, but he was quite fond of knowing they'd soon become real.

He couldn't dwell on *them*, those *other* Deities that'd ruined everything they once had. To hurt Lea like that, to betray a young child's trust, when they themselves didn't yet know any better. To go so far as to try and *kill* Lea. Lea, the youngest of them. Lea, the once most joyous and fun-loving child Deity...

Landing on the grassy knolls, Fate palmed his throbbing temple. Thank All he'd severed his red strings of fate with them—they wouldn't feel his pounding heart or his desire to tear the flesh from their throats.

As he gathered his wits, the door to the cottage swung open, and Fate was stabbed in the leg by a sword.

It might've hurt if he could die, and if the sword hadn't been made of wood. As long as the Earth kept spinning and life still flourished, Fate would be the last living thing alive. Not even Unathi, Deity of life and death, would likely be with him, though perhaps they'd die hand in hand.

As if Fate would ever touch their blood-stained hands.

He turned, lifting his robes out of the way to see little Maïmoú of Athens behind him, along with her faithful companion, her pet dog. It was a stray mutt her parents had leniently given food to. It'd stayed by Maïmoú's side ever since. Its name was Dog.

Said girl stood proudly with her wooden sword, even going so far as to hold it in the right position for a fatal blow, as Dog searched for the threat only she could see.

No fear of strangers from this one, it seemed. Fate hadn't been expecting that. He hadn't expected to see her at all. All of his visions of this day painted a very different picture. He hadn't meant for this close of contact.

Fate kept his movements slow and deliberate. He listened for her parents in the house, but he only heard the clicking of glass silverware being cleaned and put away.

He took another breath. In, then out. He regained his composure and slowed his breathing to make out a soft smile. "Hello there," he said. "How're you?"

"What're you doing on our land, trespasser?" Little Maïmoú said loudly, making Dog bark. "I'll kill you where you stand!"

As he was barraged with multiple hits to his shin and knee, Fate, taking one more look behind him, folded down his robes and took a knee. He lifted one finger in the air and gently threw the wooden sword out of Maïmoú's hand. He flung it over by the trees—little ones didn't need to bear arms.

Dog, abandoning his owner, ran to play catch.

"Huh?" Maïmoú whipped her head back and forth, spinning in a full circle to find her weapon. Her blond hair and white dress twirled like flower petals. "What did you do?"

"You seem like quite the fighter," Fate said, "but let's put our weapons down. I'm not your enemy. I'm not here to hurt you."

"You take me as a fool," she said, but her shoulders were lowering, confusion settling. Her upper lip curled to fight off reason. "I won't stand for that! I've never seen you before, so you're the enemy!"

Through his white layers, Fate couldn't feel the barrage of hits Maïmoú unleashed upon his leg. Her little fists *were* strong—they'd become stronger in just under a decade—but he didn't want her bruising. Feigning injury, Fate, being cautious of stepping over toys, led her into the long grasses.

"He's retreating!" Maïmoú called out to Dog. She smiled, all teeth. "I got you down the hill! You're defenseless!"

"Oh, yes, you got me. You're very strong, aren't you?"

"Mommy and Dadda are the strongest people ever. They're dragons, but you can't see their horns or tails. They can breathe fire, too, and fly!"

"Oh?" Fate said. "That's so impressive. Does that mean you're a dragon as well?"

"Yes! I'm the rarest dragon there is!" To prove her point, she growled and clawed at a sapling by the end of their property, bending it in half. She laughed in triumph and did a cartwheel into an anthill. Dog, who'd found the sword, ran down the hill with her. Together, the two tumbled into an embrace.

Fate tried on a nervous smile. It'd been so long since he saw a child. The last one he'd seen was Lea, but he, too, had only been a child, just mentally a few years older. Their energy was so radiant and infectious. He couldn't dare reign her in, though he didn't desire to. This little girl needed all the moments of playfulness in her subconscious as possible. But could he replicate it? Was it still in his indestructible bones to have fun? He hadn't been expecting her.

But he had. For hundreds of years, he'd known who Maïmoú of Athens would become. It was all laid out before him, maps and portraits on a cork board connected by red strings. A girl with the power to take on one half of Lea's Domain, to harness the power of humanity, *this* was her fate. Their tenacity, their ability to adapt and overcome, it all resided in her.

And he was going to be the one to destroy her. All of this, from her childhood to the fate of her parents. The world, this countryside, set ablaze because of her.

His smile fell as Maïmoú pranced in field like a newborn fawn. It had to be done—he was his Domain, through and through. Life needed hardships. People needed to suffer. Fate needed to be dealt even to the smallest, least deserving child.

The decision to crown Maïmoú a Deity when she turned thirteen would always be the hardest decision he'd ever make. He'd never once second-guessed saving Lea all those years ago. He loved her more than life itself and would do it all again in a heartbeat if it meant sparing her and the animals from death. He never questioned any of his choices, but this...

Maïmoú was but a little girl. She could live and die happily in her parent's arms until the neighboring invaders murdered them.

And she'd be with them together, that way, and might even be reincarnated hundreds or thousands of years from now. Wouldn't that be a better life than what he had in store for her?

She hadn't lived another life before this one as Maïmoú of Athens. Her first attempt at living would be drenched in heartache and blood that wasn't her own.

In, then out. He breathed in the flowers and admired the morning breeze. Soon, he'd have to deal Maïmoú this hand. He'd ruin everything just for the world to be rebuilt anew. Over and over, without purpose.

But for now...

For now, Maïmoú was happy, and that was purpose enough.

With time never on his side, Fate knelt back down to Maïmoú's level and picked a flower. "What's your favorite flower?"

Maïmoú, who was poking at an anthill, looked up. "I don't have one."

"Then which one would you like me to pick for you?"

"Huh?" She pushed through the long grasses to get back to him. Her dog, uninterested in his owner speaking to an invisible God, went to sniff the grounds for a snack. "You're picking Momma's flowers? I'm gonna tell on you!"

"These are wildflowers, not the flowers your mother planted. They're considered unwanted, but I think they're rather beautiful. They give food for bees and rabbits."

"You can't eat flowers."

"You aren't an animal. Well..." He stopped himself—a child didn't need history lessons when frolicking. "How about this?" He plucked a daisy and held it up to Maïmoú's blue eyes.

Her fingers went taut as she bit her lower lip and danced in place. "I want it!"

He gladly handed it to her. "Let me find more. Please show me how you play in the meantime."

"What's that mean?" she asked, but continued her play, cartwheeling and climbing trees with the daisy in her hair, her faithful dog barking with her joy.

Fate turned to watch her as he walked down the valley. He would've preferred speaking more to her, but speaking took a lot of effort from him. Words stuck on his tongue. His mind raced to find the best possible words to say only to mess it up, just like with everything else he touched. He learned a lot by only speaking with one person for millions of years—words were as important as memories.

He found more daisies down the hill. With a watchful eye on Maïmoú, he pocketed the best daisies he could find and paired them with complementary winter cress and dandelions. He found pliable twigs growing against stone houses and shaped them with a bit of magic. He even found brambleberries growing in a neighbor's rose patch. Forgoing the red flowers—red would soon become Maïmoú's least favorite color—he picked a handful and ate another.

When he returned to her backyard with a bitter taste in his mouth, Maïmoú was gone. He knew where she was, of course, but to anyone else, it would've taken them some time to find the little girl.

She was lying in the tall grass. Her arms and legs were outstretched as ladybugs fluttered around her knotted hair. Dog was curled up beside her, its snout resting against her heart.

"Hello again," Fate said. "Did you wear yourself out?"

Maïmoú blinked up at him, seemingly forgetting he was there. "What's that?"

With her permission, Fate knelt by her side and fanned out his robes.

Maïmoú sat back up.

"Be at peace," he said. "I'm a friend."

"I don't have friends." She picked another one of his daisies. The one he'd given her had been lost in the weeds. "What're you doing?"

"I wanted to give you a present." He began toiling with the flowers and brambles, twisting them into place. "Having friends is very important for little girls such as yourself. I know it's hard right now, but soon, you'll be matched with your perfect soulmate."

"What's a soulmate?" She scooted in closer, knees digging his robes into the dirt. "How're you doing that?"

"With practice. Practice leads to improvement, and improvement will lead to a fulfilling life. The same beliefs hold to having a soulmate. A soulmate is your other half, your forever partner. They'll transcend all barriers of an ordinary relationship and complete you wholly."

Maïmoú slapped Fate's knee, almost startling him if he didn't know her any better. She flicked the dead bug off his robes and continued listening.

Fate chuckled. "He'll be your soulmate, along with your parents. They will always be your best friends."

She cocked her curious head. "Who's 'he'? You?"

"Oh, no. I'll likely be your enemy until the Sun dies out. But for now..." He presented her her newly constructed gift.

She flinched as if he was going to hit her, then relaxed as Fate adorned her with her flower crown. Pure white and sunshine gold: the colors he and Lea associated her with.

Maïmoú tilted back as if to see the crown. She plucked a berry Fate had woven between two leaves and gave it to Dog. "Can you make me another?"

Of course, always wanting more. Such was in her nature. Such were in all of their natures. "I'm afraid I'll have to be taking my leave."

"Because you're a stranger. I can have Dadda come out here and kill you because he loves me so much."

Fate pressed his lips into a tight line. Fully the human's Deity, in time. There was no doubt about that. "I'll take your word for it. It was nice meeting you, Maïmoú."

Another cock of the head, dipping her flower crown just above her ear. "Who's Maïmoú? My name's Selene."

"Of course it is." He bowed. "Farewell, dear Selene, and keep that heart as pure as your intentions."

"You're weird." She jumped up to her bare feet and leapt back into the grass. Her dog jumped with her, tail wagging for a new adventure. "What's your name, by the way?" she asked. "So my Dadda can know."

Fate bowed once more. "I'll leave it to you to figure that out, though I'll stay in touch. I'll always be near to assist you. I'll..."

Slowly giving him the cold shoulder, Maïmoú of Athens shrugged off his concern and ran away before he could finish. She found a ball made of cow hide and lambswool and played catch all by herself.

Fate breathed in, out. He lowered his outstretched hand and tucked it back into his robes. If she'd stayed a minute longer, he would've told her that he was sorry, that if he wasn't the Deity of fate, he wouldn't do what he'd soon do to her. He'd cherish her and love her like the child she should've been left to become. So many years he'd thought about her, and he was to take away her smile like this?

So much he would've said to her, apologized for, but off she was, down the knoll to find amusement in a life he was only meant to be on the sidelines of.

And he'd be okay with that, just as he'd always been, until the end of time.

"I'll always be there for you," he finished, and disappeared for the next two millennia.

OUR DIVINE RUIN
Epilogue

At one point in his life, Shào Kǎi would've deemed himself mentally insane. A charged statement, yes, but he of all people was familiar with true insanity. His manic episodes, losing his mother, learning *how* he lost his mother, almost dying twice, being burdened to bear the sins of every known crossbreed in existence, and his fights with...

Her.

All of that would've made anyone lose their mind. *And* he was meant to, ostensibly, live forever.

With all that to say, he would've much preferred any iteration of Hell to suffer in than this tacky, piece of shit "kingdom" he'd been dropped into.

At first, he could barely open his eyes to register "where" he was. Surely, after his last fight with Maïmoú, he was once again trapped in his Void, wandering through lifeless dreams as he began healing and reliving his worst mistakes.

When he *was* finally able to open his eyes and wake from this horrid dream did he realize the nightmare had never ended.

His senses, damaged.

His body, locked in a floating, comatose state.

And his mind, utterly lost.

He was somewhere on an English coastline. That was all he could glean from his whereabouts. After his sight and senses finally crossed wires, he was able to make out the blur of sandy beaches and blue oceans. White cliff sides, crashing waves, and villages full of human beings. Just human beings, he noticed, along with some dragonborne, and a cat crossbreed, and a bird, he believed? An osprey?

He didn't know for sure. He wasn't sure of anything in this damned state. Damn his mind. His fight with Maïmoú must've been truly cataclysmic if he was trapped in a vegetative state like this. He couldn't move his fingers, blink. Faces blurred together and the Sun was too bright, so it was hard to be sure of anything anymore.

Something must've happened to the world between his fight with Maïmoú and now. The once tall skyscrapers and lit roads had now been replaced with trees and dirt, like some rogue creature had come through and taken away all progression. The land smelled different, newer, scrubbed clean of IRE-21 and the plague that'd killed so many. It reminded him of the past, and it made him sick.

Yet he couldn't even *get* sick, not in this state. For hundreds of years, Shào watched as this land dominated by humans created a new life for themselves. Without any roads or computers, beings now rode horseback and spawned royal lines from noblemen and women. They created new languages and buried any leftover technology they deemed "demonic" deep within basements and the fallout shelters still intact after so many decades.

It was medieval in nature, this new world. Their lives had reverted back to simpler times, all because of...

No one talked of the past or where they'd come from. It was like they, too, were in a state they couldn't escape from. The humans and dragons went about their lives normally, as if the amnesia Shào was experiencing was affecting them as well. Whatever had occurred during the final moments of the 22nd century, life as he knew it had disappeared and was replaced with wooden villages and cobblestone roads all trapped on this island.

But why? What had happened to the world that could affect it so? Shào had fought with Maïmoú, yes, but they couldn't have been responsible for so much change. Nor could Sabah and Tsvetan. They couldn't wipe away minds as easily as whatever devil had done so. There *was* a barrier around the island, one not even he could escape from, but was that from them?

If he was honest with himself, when Shào was this way, half-dead from an unknown assailant, he didn't care to know why. He didn't bother knowing something had permanently damaged his body or that he physically couldn't leave this strange, once established coastline. As this world slowly built itself into a homely kingdom, Shào Kǎi, Deity of crossbreeds and survivor of the most grotesque, had decided that he was tired, and he needed to rest.

He remembered his last moments as one remembered a dream. His memories up until he'd angered Maïmoú enough for her to finally try and kill him were blanked. He'd concocted a lie so cruel, it was hurtful enough for her to lay her hands on him.

"You know, I was there that morning."
"I saw the men who'd entered their home!"
"I could've saved them!"

A desperate lie. He would've added more to time had allowed it. After taking his cruel bait, she'd unleashed her fury on him with blazing eyes. It'd scared him, her sudden turn to evil. He thought, throughout everything, a small piece of her soul still loved him back. They were the fated Shào and Maïmoú. Nothing should've been able to sever that truth.

But then she must've killed him within an inch of his life, killing his crossbreeds in the process, and Earth had reverted into mundanity, simplicity. A fresh restart for the innocence they'd so casually killed.

He'd never tell her this—not like he'd ever get the chance now—but she'd actually broken one of his teeth. One of his molars, right in the back. How many people had died from that much physical pain done to his body? How many people were left, if he couldn't even leave his own mind?

He didn't care. His memories, given his sanity, were faulty at best. During the first few decades of this entrapment, he cared immensely. Screaming into his Void, he cried for anyone to help him. He banged on the walls of his mind to let him live just one more day. He couldn't say he'd been kind to his Domain, but he did miss everyday strife. Forest floors, eating real food, watching the sunrise from the Gardens' belfry with...

After two centuries of begging, Shào Kǎi had given up hope of being saved. His accumulated sins from his past had caught up to him, and he had to accept that.

After five centuries, he accepted this world as his purgatory and found solace with solitude.

But *her*. *That* girl, she stayed with him. In dreams, in nightmares, he saw her smiling. The last thing he remembered, aside from the cracked tooth and the fear, was *her*. *Her* face, as beautiful as it was demented. Her promise to end his life replayed in his head for half a millennia. To this day, he still didn't know if she'd accomplished her mission. It sure felt like it.

Being trapped in his own Void let his broken thoughts wander. He often traveled back home to his family estate. His family welcomed him back with open arms and featureless faces, showering him with an uncomplicated love he wished he'd been enough for. Dragons cuddled up with him under wisteria trees. Twilight slept on his chest like he always did.

Today's memories were somewhat tolerable. Quite often, his Void decided that he didn't deserve creature comforts and trapped him in total darkness. Not even a floor to sleep on, forcing him to float for months on end. Unable to tell how much time was passing in the real world, it could've been decades he stayed like this. It could've been minutes, and this was just the beginning to his madness.

Today, he was by a darkened lake in the middle of the forest. He often dreamt of forests as one dreamt of being murdered: it was familiar and anxiety-inducing, never knowing what lay behind a white birch or flowering wisteria.

The stars above the purpling flowers twinkled with inexplicable shine. If he focused on not dozing off for a century or two, he saw planets. He wondered if a Deity's Void was somewhere out there. If he floated up into space, would he find the Voids of the Others, of her? Would he find other earthen planets and call them his home only to burn them to ash when he was sad? Would he find the Gardens and return to an unburdened, divine life?

No. He knew that this was it, that he'd be forever bound to this prison until the end of time because of...

He didn't know. Probably *her*, the ringmaster of his heart, or perhaps the Others. They'd loved trying to mentally and emotionally abuse him to the point of suicide. If only they'd been better at it.

Crickets chirped, giving a voice to an otherwise dead forest. The hanging, purple flowers of the trees held no birds or squirrels, hid no bats or deer. At least with the deer, he'd be reminded of the Gardens and have an outlet to be depressed. Feeling anything was better than feeling nothing.

He raised a lax hand, letting his fingers thread through the hanging flowers. He swore they had a smell, even though he hadn't smelt anything since being here. Fresh and natural, with a twinge of sweetness. A blend of roasted coffee beans mixed with milk chocolate and buttery caramel...

He lifted his head. His nose twitched, sniffing the once neutral air. *Coffee.* He knew coffee. He'd walked into many coffeehouses during his decade-long manic episodes before decimating them. Beingkind had worked so hard on enriching the bean's flavor.

He turned on his side, heart racing. Why was it so strong? He hadn't been thinking about coffee—shocking no one, he preferred tea. The thought of food *had* crossed his mind, but...

In his Void, he heard voices. Dragons, he saw. He thought and felt and hated and cried until it would've destroyed most.

Since coming here, he hadn't been able to smell.

He rose above the tree line, searching the inky black sky. The scent didn't grow or lessen in intensity. It remained with him, *in* him.

"Hello?" he called out.

The sky thudded with life. The stars burst alive in a heartbeat of power. Constellations of blue and purple and yellow lit up Shào's world before it tilted.

An earthquake rumbled his mind's land. The wisteria swayed. The pond behind him splattered and dampened the world with fake water.

Shào, suspended, watched as infeasible stars burned the sky with colors. They glowed so bright, they cast shadows. Clusters of stars joined with others, creating synapses like a brain scan.

"What on *Earth*," Shào said, though he wasn't on Earth, was he? He was nowhere.

Another rumble shook him out of the sky. The air whirled him into a windstorm and sent him backwards. He yelped as he tried leashing his mind not to tug on him, but he lost control. Spinning into galaxies, Shào was thrown out of his own mind into a new darkness.

A metal pole stopped his freefall. He bent it in half, cracking his head on it with enough force that should've severed it from his shoulders. He slumped over the cool metal like hanging laundry as he painfully gathered his bearings.

It was still night time, though the sounds of forest life were replaced with a low roaring. A distant car horn and wheels skidding against...

Cars. He knew cars as well. So long had he last seen one, but nobody forgot such clever contraptions.

Peeling himself off metal, Shào looked up to the new world he'd found himself in.

He exhaled his shock. He was neither in his Void nor that pitiful kingdom of humans. His dream had reconstructed the entirety of Pangea, the city-state that'd once housed his beloved Lí, down the last molecule. He was right above the building Lí once lived in with the other soulmates. The Moon shone above the city's skyscrapers, which were still covered in trimmed bushes and trees. The scent of the coffeehouse was gone, but new scents emerged. Freshly-mowed lawns, manmade rivers and lakes. Someone in the building beneath him was cooking dinner—chicken curry and rice. He heard someone scraping a pot of rice with a rice paddle.

He pressed his back against the building's HVAC unit. Beneath him roamed ant-sized citizens in parks and walkways, walking their dogs and avoiding robots puttering down their designated paths. Life had returned to what it once was.

Shào slowly lifted himself into floating. He had to still be dreaming. Pangea had been destroyed. It'd all been laid to waste after Shào and…

He blinked back tears. He felt the night air, heard people living. An airplane, crossing the Moon's glow. Humans, crossbreeds, they'd all been brought back from the dead.

"This's too cruel." He floated off the rooftop into the open air, shamelessly letting his tears fall. This wasn't what he wanted. To be reminded of his final taste of free air, and to be sent back to where he'd lost his will to live.

When Lí had…

He'd…

Shào's head lifted, pulled upright by a force far greater and stronger than his own. His chest heaved as a string, thin as spider silk, pulled him back over the ledge.

His heart, *his* heart. Not Shào's—who cared about him—but another's. A soul more sacred than any saint or angel. That scent…

He didn't want to lose his sanity over a mere feeling, but in the past 500 years, Shào hadn't felt anything like this. Not him, not the Others, and certainly not *her*. Lí's soul had been absent

from the world and Shào had to live for the rest of eternity knowing *he* had been the cause of Lí's death.

From underneath his robes, right through his heart, a red string of fate was attached.

Shào clutched the start of the string. The glistening thread materialized out of thin air and wrapped around the building's HVAC unit. Around vents and antennae, on the other side of the building—

"Lí?"

He couldn't rationalize it. He couldn't breathe, though his body no longer had to. Standing alone on the rooftop, turning to find someone himself, was him. His Lí, looking up at Shào like he'd been waiting for him all this time. He still had his shaggy hair, his same oversized, second-hand clothes he was so modest to wear. His scuff, his fingerless gloves: This was his Lí.

A thousand words, a million apologies and justifications. It all hit Shào at once, until he was speechless, an unworthy believer before his God. He gulped down nothing in a too-dry mouth and he wavered in a sky whose gravity didn't affect him. *Nothing*, he was nothing. He had nothing and could give nothing to the one soul who deserved everything.

"Lí," Shào repeated, breathless. "Lí, is that truly you?"

"Yeah," Lí said, though he didn't make another move. He was just as speechless to have crossed paths with *his* God.

Shào's body, conspiring with his heart, moved against his will. He floated down to Lí's level, touched his cheek. The coarse hair from days of not shaving, and his cologne. He was real and alive and Shào had been given one boon after a lifetime of misery.

Hugging Lí was like hugging him for the first time. He smelled of memories and felt like home. Shào inhaled into his shoulder so his brain would never, ever forget him. As if he ever could. They were soulmates.

"Oh, Lí," Shào said, tears welling. "How I've missed you so."

A beat, a shared heartbeat between two boys, and Lí pushed Shào back, palming him in the chest to get them to separate. Shào jumped back, ready to please him to the end of the Earth, but the man before him now was no longer his Lí.

Shào's brain lagged like an overheating computer. Standing in Lí's place was now a girl. Short, small—she was about a few years older than him—with dark skin and coiled hair. She was a rat crossbreed, so she had two pink rat ears and a beige, thin tail, and...

She was perfect. Absolutely stunning, from her buck teeth to her scuffed basketball shoes. Shào couldn't breathe or dare move before her, for no one else, aside from Lí, could affect him in such a way that made him want to live again.

Shào tried swallowing again. Lí was dead. There was no getting him back. Shào had failed him.

But the reincarnation cycle, and his red string of fate. He touched it, materializing it back into reality. It was going through the girl's chest now, though she made no move to see it herself. They were one in the same. They were...

"Who are you?" the girl asked. "What's going on?"

That *language*. A mix of several across time and countries, unlike anything he'd ever heard.

Except one. "You speak the same language the humans do?" he asked. The people in that confusing "Drail Kingdom," memories wiped and begun anew.

The more important question: "Who are you?"

"I asked you first," the girl said. She was so blunt, harkening back to how Lí was in his final years. "I was just sleeping on my aunts' roof when I woke up here. Where am I? This isn't anywhere in Raeleen."

Shào went to read her mind to get his answers, but his mind wasn't focusing. Lí's heart, his drive, it was all beating inside this girl. "Did you arrive with the osprey as well?" he asked. If he honed in on his thoughts, he remembered seeing a flighted crossbreed in that kingdom. He'd arrived just days ago, or had it been weeks? "Are you in the Drail Kingdom?"

The girl's tail twitched. "Stop asking questions about me. Where am I?"

So bold. Was this truly Lí in another body? Did he still hate the person Shào had become for him? Shào regretted a lot of his life, but what he'd done to Lí had been his worst regret. That and—

"I'm making myself wake up."

Shào started. Whatever was happening, wherever he and this girl were, Lí had been given a second chance, and Shào couldn't lose him again.

"Don't!" He grabbed hold of her arm. She was warm. "Please, don't leave. I'm sorry. I haven't conversed with someone in hundreds of years. I'm simply perplexed by this meeting and who...you are."

The girl's body tensed. Shào loosened his grip but refused to let go. "What's your name this time?"

"This time?" the girl asked. "Nikki. Nicole Lenore."

And Shào fell.

Deeper and deeper.

Until he was lost.

Intoxicated by all of Lí's mind and body—of Nicole's—Shào lost himself to yet another soulmate and their charming soul.

They must've been speaking, for he saw her mouth moving. And since she kept talking and engaging with someone as unworthy as he, he must've been responding with enough intelligence to keep the conversation going, but what they were discussing was lost to him. He was drinking in every ounce of Nicole Lenore like he'd be tested on her taste. He didn't care if he'd truly gone insane and this was his mind's way of easing him into another decade-long slumber. Knowing Lí's soul had once again graced his life would give him enough purpose to want to live another lifetime.

And things would be different this time. If Fate, whoever he was, thought Shào deserved a second chance in the form of this brilliant girl, he'd take it to heart. No harm would ever come to her. He'd devote his life to her, body and soul. She'd live a long and happy life this time, and he'd break free of this bodily tomb and find her and love her the way he once deserved.

"Shào?"

Her saying his name brought him back. She'd been telling him about who she was and where she resided in the world. He didn't know for sure—he'd been getting lost in her ruby red eyes. She was looking up at him with lips parted and...

And...

Shào's pointed ears flicked. While basking in the light that was Nicole Lenore, he'd lost his sense of fight or flight, permanently broken by *her*.

Her.

Her.

His hair stood on end, the electricity frying the once calm, night air. He floated higher to see beyond the buildings. Damn the once future citizens using the most energy-efficient lighting to light their damn city-state—all he had was the Moon's glow to find...

"She's here," he whispered, and prayed to every last God and patron saint that he was wrong. He'd asked for a boon, not a double-edged sword.

"Who?" Nikki asked.

Shào dug a hand into Nikki's soft shoulder. This gut-wrenching feeling of guilt and fear was that of an animal ready to bite.

His eyes locked on a building across the lake. Dull balls of light lit up the roof terrace around perfectly-planted hedges and patio umbrellas, and standing atop an antenna, waving like a billowing white flag, was her.

Her.

Her.

"Maïmoú."

The curse left his lips before he could stop it. Maïmoú of Athens, like Lí's perfect soul, had once again returned to the timeline.

Shào licked his lips, anticipating, fearing. She was so far away, but he saw her clear as day. Her blond hair caught in the night air. Her blue eyes were as bright as the Gardens' moons. It looked like she was trying to speak. He yearned to hear one single word.

Shào squeezed Nikki's shoulder harder and readied for another fight of his life. Both of them might've been brought back to life, and he might not be truly corporeal in the timeline yet, but one of them wasn't leaving this dream alive.

"I'm sorry," Shào said to Nikki, and then he, like before, like always, until the end of this doomed timeline, went to blast Maïmoú of Athens off the face of the Earth.

THEIR FATES UNDONE
Prologue

———————◆ ☾ ◆———————

Fate would never forget the day their fates changed for the worse. It'd not only been their fates that'd suffered the repercussions, but also the world, and every single being that had yet to be thought into creation. Things could've played out so differently, if they'd only listened to her.

It'd been overcast in the Gardens that fateful day, their favorite type of weather, and Ataleah had been gone for weeks. That girl couldn't keep away from Earth for too long, even though Fate, Sabah, Tsvetan, and Unathi had worked tirelessly on making these Gardens beautiful. Their own little world, a pocket dimension between the real and the fabricated. Fate had discovered the world in a dream, and together, with his friends, they'd created their playground.

The Gardens had been smaller back then, only a fraction of what it would become. The towers were still tall, piercing through the clouds, and the plots of land were still verdant with life. They had a mere dozen buildings and only a hundred or so rooms all connected by stone walkways. But it was all so fresh, so new. He saw the plans for something greater all laid out in his mind, but the invisible papers were overlapping, confusing him on the true path set for them.

"Just leave her be, Fayfay," Sabah said from her side of the balcony. She, Tsvetan, and Fate were together that morning—they were always together, even back then—enjoying the cool winds of Sabah's Domain.

Fate was tucked in the corner, giving Sabah more space to work. She was picking out her favorite shells she and Unathi had collected on the eastern shorelines that week and was embedding them into the railing. Back then, her hair barely reached past her twelve-year-old shoulders. Her blue eyes weren't as heavy. "She'll just tire herself out in a few years, then she'll come crawling back like always."

"We shouldn't be letting her roam about Earth alone," Fate said. "She's just a baby."

Sabah mocked his tone and continued decorating. They'd all been living in these Gardens for centuries, but Fate and their friends couldn't help but change their world every millennium or so. They'd topple down spires and bridges just to terraform the entire northern side of the Gardens for fun. Sabah loved decorating the exteriors. Tsvetan loved his indoor and outdoor plants, of course, and Unathi loved aesthetics above all else. They made the buildings gleam and the windows glimmer in rainbows. Anything could happen in their world. It was their dominion, after all.

Fate frowned and waited for his friends to care more than he did, but he should've known, even back then.

"I miss her," Fate said.

"Then go find her yourself!" Tsvetan said. He was sitting on the balcony railing by Sabah, kicking his feet as he admired her work. "You seem to love her so much, why don't you do that thing you said we'd do in a billion years with her? What was the word? We'd *marry* each other?"

Sabah snorted. "That's such a weird word," she said. "Are you sure we'd do something like that?"

"You know my visions aren't exact," Fate mumbled.

"If I ever wanted to," Tsvetan said, ignoring him, "I'd just stay with the three of you forever. We already do that, even before silly Ataleah came into existence."

Fate ignored him back and gave them the cold shoulder. He didn't even bother explaining himself and his mysterious Domain to them anymore. Whenever his mind wandered, the visions came to him. Possible futures and outcomes depending on how stable the Earth wanted to be. They were uncertain, blurry like polluted water, but the colors he saw? The possibilities? He thought it was the most magical experience. His head would fuzz over, sometimes becoming too unbearable to deal with, but he saw so many incredible things.

But what was he met with? Whenever he came to them with his visions, they shunned him. They called him weird. While their Domains were so straightforward, the obscure, the undefined, scared them. The only person who did understand him, who took the time to hear him out and get excited for change, was...

A teleportation between Fate and the Others brought him out of his head. Unathi, panting, jumped onto the balcony, their long, white dress catching in the stormy breeze.

The look in their golden eyes sank Fate's stomach. It was true Fate didn't know everything that was going to happen—they couldn't even see the paths set by their friends—and that made him nauseous with fear of the unknown. Seeing Unathi worried about anything was a rarity these days. Out of all of them, they were the most composed.

Unathi signed to Sabah and Tsvetan. "There's something wrong."

"With what?" Fate asked.

Tsvetan and Sabah jumped to their feet and tended to their distraught friend. Fate stayed back, trying to read Unathi's tense body language.

Unathi signed quickly. "There's something happening on Earth. I don't know. My stomach is all twisted up inside like I'm—"

They stopped signing to hold a hand to their mouth. They keeled over and heaved, and Sabah and Tsvetan consoled their dearest friend.

"Is it Ataleah?" Fate asked, and subtly touched the invisible threads spilling out of their heart. They had millions and millions of ties across the world, from plants to animals to the Earth itself, but he easily found Ataleah's. It was taut but not painfully so. It was as bright as blood.

"What did she do this time?" Sabah said, and cast a look into her own skies. In the distance, beyond the untouchable mountains, storm clouds were rolling in. Back then, her emotions were so tied to her Domain, cataclysmic storms would ravage the world on her worst days. "Tantan, let's go."

"O-okay," he said, unwilling to disagree with his leader, and together, with Fate following from behind, the four of them teleported into the real world.

Fate didn't know why the Others hated Earth. Earth had been their cradle. Fate didn't remember when or how or where or why, but they remembered crawling out of its wet dirt and soil. They remembered how cold it was, how there was little to no oxygen in the air, and how lonely he'd been. It'd taken a few centuries for the Others to come, and then even more time for Ataleah to come. He'd been the first to witness all of Earth's divine beauty. Deities didn't have to breathe, but now, surrounded by water and life, Fate had trouble imagining Earth without them.

They teleported to where they felt Ataleah lingering. She'd been staying in one forested grove for those last few weeks, a patch of flowers surrounded by evergreen trees as tall as mountains. As soon as they entered the space, the life of the forest tweeted and trilled at them in greeting. The tiniest animals—dinosaurs, as they'd later be called—scampered across the grass to hide in the ferns. Down by a nearby stream, the first of what would later be called prehistoric crocodiles were sunbathing between pockets of light.

Ataleah was on the ground. What had once been a valley of wildflowers had been reduced to dirt and mud like a pack of wild beasts had trodden down the land. Trees had been cut in half and were lying across thick vines able to hold up their weights.

When Ataleah saw them, she smiled. One of her juvenile front teeth was missing, and she waved to her friends to come nearer. "Guys, guys! Look at what I made!"

The Others, unmoving, instead took in the land Ataleah had destroyed. Her hands were caked in dried dirt like she'd bathed in it, and her dark brown hair was more of a rat's nest than ever before. Fate would have to brush it out for her. She was just a baby.

Blood soaked her skinned knees and feet. Through the mud, wet blood was smeared across the upturned roots of Tsvetan's trees. Despite the morbid scene, Ataleah beamed as she got up too quickly and pushed back her matted strands of hair. "Look!"

The creature in her dirty hands was small, scaled, and beady-eyed. It looked like a baby crocodilian, with its sharp tail and sharper teeth, but this creature was coated in red scales. Its limbs were too long, its horns too deadly.

Its wings, bat-like and skin-soft, were folded across Ataleah's hands as she showed them what had to be a new species of animal.

"Ataleah," Fate breathed. "What...is that?"

"He's my new friend!" she exclaimed. "I just made him. I took the blood of this animal and that, then mixed it with my blood—"

"You what?" Sabah asked. "What do you mean?"

"No, listen!" Ataleah moved closer to show them what she saw.

Everyone but Fate backed up.

"It's just like us!" she said. "Look!"

She tossed the animal into the air, this small, fragile creature who'd just been born, or created. It spun in loose circles above their heads. As the Others screamed and ducked away in fear, only Fate and Ataleah watched the creature take its first breath of life.

Fate watched, astonished, as the creature blew out the hottest, whitest fire he'd ever seen. It scorched the evergreen branches as a plume of dark matter stole it away from the world and disappeared it back into Ataleah's arms.

Ataleah spun around, giggling as she caught the beast, the dragon, Fate realized. Upon seeing the fearsome, new creature of the world, Fate experienced a wave of information just now unlocked by Ataleah.

He held back his head from leaking all over the forest floor. Dragons, lizards, divinity within animals. Dragonborne, monkeys, cities, pain. Legs going numb, he fell to the dirtied, bloody ground and lost his focus. Visions of the future warped around him. His ears thrummed with possibility. His white cloak was getting soaked in red.

"See?" Ataleah asked triumphantly. "Isn't it neat? I'm calling it a dragon, and I have ideas for a bunch of other dragons that can do the same kinda magic we can do! Isn't it cool? Do you like it?"

Fate didn't look at the Others, who'd all run away behind a fallen tree so they didn't get hit by any fire or dark matter or whatever other magic this creature could do. Magic, fires, slavery, evil.

From the way Ataleah's animated face fell, the way she dropped the animal to her side and held it like a wilted rose, told Fate just how the Others were handling this profound change.

Ataleah let the dragon squirm out of her grip and thrash on the ground. "What's wrong?" she asked. "Don't…don't you like it?"

"Ataleah, what is that?" Sabah repeated. "Kill it. It's unnatural!"

"But why?" She pouted, her small cheeks reddening in anger. "I made it. It's part of my Domain. Aren't you proud?"

"It'll ruin my Domain," Tsvetan said. "It's too powerful."

"And it'll mess up my oceans!" Sabah added.

Unathi must've signed something, because Ataleah's eyes tracked down. Or maybe she was no longer looking at the people she just wanted to impress.

"It's a monster," Sabah said. "Just like *you*."

Tears welled in Ataleah's red eyes. She stepped from foot to foot, unsure of what to say next. "But…but I just wanted…"

Fate held his head. Dragons, beingkind, shifting world politics. Slavery, redemption, cities being conquered. So many visions flashed by in his mind, but he tried blocking it all out. Struggling, he got to his hands and knees and crawled to Ataleah.

"You weren't thinking," Sabah said. "How many more did you make?"

"I-I don't know. A few. Don't you like them, though? They're just like us."

"Nothing can be like us!" Sabah exploded. "You're so stupid, Ataleah! Why don't you ever think things through? How big can that thing get? How smart can it get? You can't keep *doing* this, Ataleah. Come on!"

Ataleah stepped back on the dragon's tail, making it cry out. She flinched and held herself back as her confused tears muddied the Earth.

Fate fought to his feet and turned to face his friends. "Don't...don't call Ataleah stupid."

A splash of water hit him in the face. Ice cold, it pushed him down and washed Ataleah to her bare feet. Instantly, she went to the dragon and scooped it back up, sheltering it from abuse.

Sabah, Tsvetan, and Unathi were running away from the grove, Tsvetan wailing, Sabah cursing. They left Fate and Ataleah in the mud in fear of something they'd just met and with no knowledge of its future potential.

Ataleah curled her head into Fate's back. He let her cry into him, holding her with trembling arms as he kept from overthinking what on Earth this little girl had just done to the world.

Fate hadn't stopped walking for years. For how many, he wouldn't begin to count. He'd tried for centuries and it only made himself crazy.

A million years. Ten million years. On and on he walked in this limitless Void, though there had to be a limit. Even if none of the Others had ever bothered to find one, Fate knew nothing was endless. Everything had an end. Whether it was a happy one or not would be up to him.

"She's a monster!"

His friends' words haunted him as he walked, whispering into his ears.

"Look at what she's done! First those dragons, and now these monkeys! We couldn't let her keep doing this. You've told us how our fates can change if she grows too powerful. What other choice did we have?"

Fate stared straight ahead as he walked. When his eyesight started doubling, he swore he saw those friends walking beside him.

"This's all your fault! If you weren't such a pushover, you could've stopped her!"

"We had to take it into our own hands."

"I'm sorry, Fate, but you gave us no choice."

He couldn't remember how much time had passed between then and now. He couldn't remember what he'd said to make them snap like that, but once they did, everything unraveled. Once they told Fate the truth about what they'd done...

"We had no choice!"

As if they needed to lecture him on his own Domain.

They'd grown older since Ataleah had made the very first dragon. They'd grown into young adults and Ataleah had been a bright teenager. Asteroids had come, just as Fate predicted, weakening all of them, disappearing them to their Voids for hundreds of years. They'd returned bruised but alive, ready to continue the fight of living.

But then the sicknesses came. Ataleah's beautiful animals had suffered so greatly. Extinction after extinction, her Domain was dying, and Fate couldn't understand why. Why were the waters so polluted? Why were the roots poisoned? Sabah and Tsvetan had gotten sick from it, too, but all those poor animals, Fate couldn't understand what was happening.

Until that day.

"We had no choice!"

Fate wiped his eyes that were still raw from crying. Ataleah had disappeared into her Void, and this time, she didn't return. Clueless, Fate had gone to his friends, his trusted friends, his *family*, to ask them for help. A Deity's mind was so expansive, but if all of them went in to try and find her, maybe they could bring her back.

None of them volunteered. Sabah swept his concern under the rug. Unathi stopped talking to him. In a fit of rage, Fate had confronted all of them, begging for the truth.

And he got it. The truth he was so certain would never happen, *could* never happen, had, and all under his nose, too. A betrayal of not only Fate's trust but Ataleah's as well, the youngest of them all.

And so, that night, when all of them were asleep in the Gardens, after Sabah admitted to slowly poisoning Ataleah over the last million years to kill her, Fate walked out to the Gardens' mountains and never returned.

On and on he went, walking through the vastness of his own mind, to find the last Deity on Earth who mattered to him.

Ataleah wasn't "on" Earth the same way that possibility wasn't, but the metaphor still stuck. Fate knew she was somewhere separate from them, healing after her creatures had almost been eradicated. The only way to find her now was through the Void.

He'd just wished, once he'd entered his Void, that his friends had stopped him. Tsvetan or Unathi would call his name for him to come back home, or Sabah would touch his shoulder and apologize for what she'd done. They'd grown up for billions of years together. They had a history no other creatures on Earth had.

She hadn't come. None of them had. The Others had chosen to let Ataleah fade away as a bitter yet forgotten memory.

Fate kept walking through the stark whiteness of his Void. He would no longer be that pushover for Ataleah's sake. He was a man now, and he'd seen them hit her, poison her Domain by spiking their own with toxins. They'd destroyed their own ecosystems to try to rid the world of animals and dragons. All because they feared her powers becoming greater than their own, as if they couldn't live with the fact that the youngest had outplayed them.

Fate had tried to stop them, but three against one had never been a fair fight. All his efforts to preserve Ataleah's fragile state, all the words he yelled at them, the threats of the possible future...

He kept walking, searching. They knew what they'd been doing. From the day Ataleah showed her potential, they sought to eat her away like carnivorous insects.

When he let his mind wander like this, focusing on the what-ifs, he had to sit down. His Void was a slate of white, a grey, blurry streak marking the horizon as his only viewpoint. He'd been staring at it for centuries as he searched for her. Before he realized it, he'd fallen, his white robes fanning out across the mirrored floor.

His mind spun. Separated from the world like this had untethered him from reason. He yearned to be back home. His body craved solutions.

His heart wanted to be torn out by the Others.

Fighting the urge to vomit on invisible floors, Fate picked himself up and continued on.

He had to stop. Every other week, every new month that began and ended, he needed to rest. He wasn't necessarily tired, but when he realized he was spinning in tight circles, he had to lie down.

Within a Deity's Void, you were resting. You were asleep or dreaming or, if injured, you were healing. You disappeared from the world to fix your mind. If all things had gone correctly, not even his body should've been left in the world. He'd left the Others without a word, and they'd be left in confusion for the rest of time.

Because Fate wasn't going back. Even if he did find Ataleah in this collective dreamport, which he knew he would, statistically, he wasn't going back to those thieves of happiness.

In his Void, he dreamt of Earths. Better Earths, optimistic possibilities skyrocketing Earthen life into their futures. He saw humanity and crossbreeds, two species that would become very important in later centuries. He knew they'd come, just like he knew that he'd find Ataleah.

He just had to be better.

Work harder.

And find her.

He hated them. He hated the way his own friends, people whom he'd struggled to see in a better light, thought abusing Ataleah, a *child*, would make her submit to them. He hated how they feared her enough to bully her when his back was turned. He hated Tsvetan's meekness, Sabah's authority, and Unathi's indifference.

Most of all, Fate hated the way he'd let it get to that point. He didn't know. Truly, he didn't. He knew Sabah, Tsvetan, and Unathi well enough and knew that deep down, there was a part of them that knew when to stop. The paths in his head had told him so. In certain outcomes, they'd realize their errors, beg for her forgiveness, and they'd all become closer as a true family.

He knew Ataleah wouldn't change. Growing up, while he hadn't been afraid of Ataleah, he knew her temper would lead her down dark paths. Violence came as naturally as love did, two sides of an extreme none of them knew how to regulate. Because Fate saw this all, he'd tried finding middle ground between All.

The dreams dragged him down, back into memories he dared not relive. Ataleah had created creatures out of drawings done in mud and clay, willing them to life over the course of hundreds of years. It took Tsvetan double the time to make a flower change its natural colors. She was unstoppable, inspiring.

The Others, they'd never seen it that way.

"You're not doing enough."

"You won't ever find her."

"Give up, and go back, and forget about her."

Fate thrashed on the invisible ground as panicked dreams startled him awake. He couldn't tell how long he'd been asleep. He didn't even remember lying down.

All he knew was that he had to keep going, and keep searching, for her.

Because there was no going back, he feared, for there was nothing left for him on Earth.

Time was passing, and Fate didn't know how to handle the change.

He and the Others aged slower than any other being on Earth. They wouldn't notice each other growing older until one of them pointed it out. A dip in their voice. A new mole on their back. Tsvetan's hills sloped into mountains and Sabah's oceans swallowed islands whole and not a year would pass them, not physically. Unathi had guessed that a day for them was thousands of millions of years for animals, but it might've been even longer.

When Fate awoke to a scratchy chin, he thought he'd truly gone insane, imagining bugs crawling up and down his robes or a rash spreading across his body. When he looked down at his mirror self and found the stubble growing, he'd frozen in place.

While he was in his late twenties, he'd had trouble growing facial hair. Tsvetan had no trouble with it. Why they needed it in the first place perplexed him—a Deity was infertile, so they had no need for sexual dimorphism. He knew humans and crossbreeds would come to have it, but...

He'd never been in his own Void for this long. Back on Earth, he was missing out on millions of years of evolution and growth for *all* of their Domains. What was happening to the world now that the Deity of fate was absent? A number of things, from the world collapsing in on itself to absolutely nothing. Anything was possible in his mind's eye. That was his curse, being this Deity of chance: He knew thousands of possibilities for millions of circumstances, and the way a butterfly beat its wings could change it all.

He kept walking even when he could no longer feel his feet. He kept calling for her even when his voice no longer worked.

He had to find her.

He owed her that much.

And when his legs wouldn't move, he crawled. For hundreds of miles, he kept looking for her.

He dropped his hand over his eyes. Tears cascaded down his cheeks. His head hurt. His body hurt. He couldn't keep going. He'd fail Ataleah, just like he'd failed her so many times in her short life. Now she'd die, because of him.

Something kicked his arm. It took a few more kicks for him to register the touch and look over his shoulder.

Sabah stood over him. She was much younger than when he'd left her, a child with her arms defiantly on her hips. "You're giving up *now*? I know you're a pushover, Fayfay, but this is just sad."

Fate dropped his arms to stare at the child before him. It'd been millions of years since he'd seen her like this.

Two others appeared behind her, hidden behind their fierce protector. Tsvetan had his hair long and pinned back with purple flowers. Unathi held Sabah's shoulder as they looked over at Fate with a gentle smile that'd once won over Fate.

"Why's he on the ground?" Tsvetan asked Sabah.

"Maybe he's hurt," signed Unathi.

"Maybe he's just a baby," said Sabah casually. "You know how he is. He barely tries, and then he gives up when he doesn't get his way."

That wasn't true. He was always trying. They never saw that side of him because they were better friends with each other than they ever had been with him.

"He's different from us. He doesn't know how to fight for his own Domain."

Agitated colors swirled above them. Maybe he *did* want to give up and bury his head in the ground. Just for a few thousand years. He'd be stronger then.

"Unless," Sabah said, "he wants to prove us wrong."

Fate breathed in, then out. In, then out. He then rolled over to his side and struggled to his sandaled feet.

Sabah huffed indignantly and stepped aside. "Looks like the loser's up," she said. "Come on, Fayfay. Show the world what you still have left."

The three children stepped back to let him through. He'd continue on his hands and knees until he could no longer bear it, then keep going a little longer, just to spite Sabah. Call it childish. He didn't care. They were all still children at heart.

The phantom children disappeared in clouds of sparkling dark matter. He coughed to keep it out of his lungs, and when he looked back up, a new figure formed against the grey horizon line.

For a moment, he thought it was a pile of dirty laundry. Much to the Others' annoyance, Fate wasn't a stranger to leaving piles of his robes in whatever part of the Gardens they decided to call home for that century. But he hadn't conjured up such a frivolous idea. He barely had any energy to see straight.

He certainly hadn't created the large wolf looming over the pile of laundry. Its body shimmered and faded against the snow-white background, its darkness flecked by dark matter. Normally, dark matter flowed like watery mud, bending to the will of the

Deity in control of it. The only one of them that liked conjuring it into shapes was...

Any and all pain Fate was experiencing vanished. His feet slam down on the ground hard enough to crack it as he ran for her.

The old, dirty clothes were in the shape of a girl. He saw hidden fingers bitten down and bloody, hair matted and dirty. A boot, a feathered necklace, all hidden within the folds of starchy fabric.

As Fate knelt down, the wolf, which was much skinnier than any creature should've been, bowed its head before fading into nothingness, its duty as her guardian fulfilled.

"Ataleah." Fate's fingers shook as he carefully unfolded the layers. It couldn't have been a mirage, but some part of his brain knew it could've been. She wasn't answering him. He couldn't see her.

He backed up, just an inch. Instinctive revulsion swept through him. Ataleah was skin and bones. Her face was gaunt. Her red eyes were sunken in. Her lips were pulled back from either dehydration or illness, and by the way her head sagged, one would've assumed she was a corpse.

"Ataleah." He picked her up and held her close. He felt her heart beat against him, but it wasn't in sync. She had no life in her.

A hand. So light, so gentle, like snowfall. Two fingers touched the small of his back in welcome.

He cracked apart as tears fell from both of their eyes. She moaned incoherently as another living being touched her for the first time in millions of years. Fate held her head, petting her, telling her not to move or speak or do anything but breathe. She couldn't afford it like this.

Another hand found his back and gripped it tight, tearing out stitches. She used whatever was left inside her to pull herself against him and weep. Fate tried finding it in him not to collapse with her—he hadn't fought all this way to lose her to his own inabilities.

After what felt like hours spent like that, Fate dared to move, to see her once more and know that this wasn't another hallucination.

Ataleah didn't let him. Her grip on him was like a knife pressed to his back, daring him not to breathe.

"Why?" she croaked out, her voice pained. "*Why?*"

"I-I don't know," he sputtered. "I don't know. I'm sorry. I'm sorry I couldn't come sooner. I'm sorry it got to this point, my love. A million times over, I'm sorry."

"It hurts."

The words struck him harder than any asteroid. "I know. I'm sorry."

"It hurts so much. I can't breathe."

"I know. I'm sorry."

"They...they did this, didn't they?"

"They did."

"Like you warned."

"I should've done more to stop them, I know. I'm sorry."

"But...you came?"

He sighed into tears. "Yes. I came. You're in my Void, my darling girl. I won't leave. You'll heal faster here. I'm sure of it."

"Don't go?" She said it as a question, but he knew it better as a demand poised to be answered.

"I won't," he said. "I'll do right by you this time. I'll never leave you, Ataleah. I'll stay."

Her sharp nails cut through his robes and into his pale, tattooed skin. He felt his own blood run down the length of his back as Ataleah shook with raw emotion.

Anger. Hatred. Her lips let loose a snarl into Fate's shoulder as she shivered with an animalistic heat.

"I'll kill them," she promised the world. "Each of them, one by one, for this. Mark it. Ink it. I will eat them whole for this."

Fate kept patting the back of Ataleah's head, running his hands through the knots he'd take care of undoing for her. "Of course, my love," he said sweetly. "I will help you undo them. I'll stay with you for it and every step next. Always," he promised.

And promise he did.

THEIR FATES UNDONE
Epilogue

Wren hadn't meant to be late—his alarm didn't go off, and his parents *knew* he had trouble getting up at the sound of bird calls, even if he'd grown up in a family comprised mostly of airborne.

Not that he still needed his parents to wake him up, but he knew he'd get an earful when he went downstairs. How much depended on who he'd see first.

He tried keeping his footfalls light as he swiftly got ready for the day. It wasn't an issue for him—since he'd been a young teen, he'd shared a room with his two younger siblings, Mako and Nina, a human boy and airborne respectively, both of whom were still asleep in their beds. Their parents, while nowhere near as coinless as they'd been when Wren was a kid, still didn't have the means to give each of their kids their own bedroom. Wren couldn't say he hated it, but he was counting the days he'd get his own bedroom.

He rustled each of their little heads as he got dressed. He made his bed so his parents wouldn't be cross with him, gathering all the blankets and pillows he'd kicked off in his sleep. As he cleaned, he found Dolly stuck between his bedpost and writing desk. His most favorite toy, an old rag doll made by a family friend. It was so old, his aunt had to stitch it up every time she came back home from her trips across the world. He'd thought about getting rid of it, but it held too many memories, and dollies were important. Smiling, he placed Dolly back on his pillow, fixing her dress and brushing out her yarn hair.

He brushed out his own dark hair while humming, keeping his movements quick and calculated. His parents' room was just across the hall, and he had tenants, or neighbors, to his left and right. He lived in an old inn some human lady once owned. After she died, she'd given the house to one of the tenants, who then entrusted it to Wren's dad once they moved down to Costashire. Now, just a few families lived with them, but Wren believed they'd soon own the whole inn in another few years. *Then* he'd get his own room.

After moistening his skin and gills with lubricating waterborne lotion, Wren tiptoed down the hall and onto the first step of the stairs.

The ancient wood betrayed him, creaking his entire weight throughout the building. It took seconds after he reached the first floor before he heard it.

"Wren? That you?"

His heart dropped as he ran for the back doors. While he and his mom were the same species, Wren hadn't enrolled in both the track and field team *and* swim team for four years for nothing. Waterborne needed to harden their endurance, especially those who'd been born in the Asilo.

Not that Wren had memories of the Asilo. Stepping outside in the fresh spring air, he couldn't imagine how people like his mom grew up in such awful conditions.

He *was* thankful he didn't remember where he was born, but he did have...feelings. When the adults talked about Raeleen and the guards and the treatments they'd undergone, he smelled iron-rich saltwater. He felt the trapping glass against his palms and tasted food he couldn't find in Drail. Luckily, the senses faded as soon as he focused on them, like a dream that ended too soon.

He wondered, at times, if they were his own memories, or if he was trying to reminisce about a life that'd been described to him from strangers. His mom never talked about it unless he brought it up, and his dad never talked about anything more upsetting than the weather these days. He had his own memories that were impossible to work through.

Wren tripped over the stone path that wound through their backyard garden. According to his dad, crossbreeds back in the day didn't know a lot about gardening. They had labs to make most of their food. Looking at his dad, Wren wouldn't have known he wasn't born with a trowel in hand.

His dad was hidden in his garden of leaves and vines, speaking with his neighbors across the river. With Wren about to leave the nest, his dad was spending most of his free time tending to their tiny farm. Fat potatoes, carrots the length of his dad's tail feathers, redberries, blueberries, even the occasional head of lettuce, though Wren hated it, and flowers. So many vibrant flowers, it made him get hay fever every year. He didn't complain. His mom told him to be grateful for what they had, no matter the cost.

His dad bid the neighbors farewell, then groaned as he cracked his back. He used one of his large wings to block the morning Sun from his eyes. "Oh. Morning, Wren. Did you wake up late again?"

"You make it sound like I'm *always* late." He side-stepped around the garden patches, nudging closer to the garden gates. "I went to bed late last night, that's all. Lexi and Juni have a massive project due next Monday that I'm helping them on, and I have finals."

"Then shouldn't you be studying instead of getting roped in to helping them?" He took off his gloves with his teeth and handed Wren a handful of freshly-picked redberries, which Wren gobbled down in one bite. "You shouldn't let them be so dependent on you. Co-dependence with anything isn't good."

"I know, I know, but it's easy work. Stuff I learned years back. That's why I tried heading out early, but here I am, stuck yapping with you."

"Because you're already *so* late?" He cocked his head to their home, his long ponytail swaying between his wings. "You have about three seconds before—"

"Wren!"

Wren ran. He tried not slamming the garden gate, for the chickens. They had a habit of getting spooked into the trees, and it bothered his dad enough to make a habit of throwing them himself. One got close, but his dad was too distracted to notice.

Wren's mom came out through the back door, ready to scold her son for very regular behavior for an eighteen-year-old, but she was smiling. She had Wren's recently-adopted sister attached to her back in a protective sling. She was a rat crossbreed, Clara, and made so much noise, any babble could've been labeled as speech.

His mom waved to his dad, warm as the springtime sun. "Wren! Dovie! Come here, I think she said it!"

His dad started out of his garden. "No way. What did she say? Which one was it?"

"I'm pretty sure it was, '*momma*', but I wasn't paying attention."

His dad laughed. "She's only five months old! That's incredible!"

Wren didn't stick around to see what babble his mom was interpreting as speech. She did that with every kid, fawning over every burp and snot bubble they made. He remembered how she used to congratulate him on every single thing he did as a kid. It kept him away most days, deciding to spend more time with friends than with his own parents. And they were just babies.

But by the sound of his mom's and dad's laughter, they must've been being embarrassing again. Even when they were so old and kind of dull, whenever they thought Wren wasn't looking, they'd be kissing and hugging like they were teenagers again. Not even Wren did stuff like that.

Not that Wren was a late bloomer. No matter what the girls said, he was the most perfectly average man.

Thinking about that too much made him run even faster. Grateful as he was for his family, he was glad they let him spread his metaphorical wings on the weekends.

The forest was awake with life. His neighbors were out tending to their own gardens, sharing with families, walking their dogs. A herd of goats nibbled on wild grass while their owners, a goat crossbreed family, watched from their patio. Most of their neighbors were crossbreeds, but a few humans had rooted themselves in Fleetwood. There had to be over twenty houses out here now, and there were more on the way. His dad's twin had made a name for themselves with their mate, Oliver, and their lodging company.

If Wren squinted through the trees, he could see their company working deeper into the trees, sawing down what was once a thick forest to make more homes. It was always easy to spot their dad's twin siblings's giant wings.

Wren broke through the trees and took off down the road. How he wished he had a bike or a hoverboard like the richer kids had. He wasn't as lucky as the girls in that regard.

His view was better than theirs, though. He and his parents lived on the outskirts of Fawnfield and weren't bothered by the commotion of town life. The church bells were always going off, and the giant windmills were noisy during these spring months. They'd recently installed three mills around Fawnfield, towering pillars with fifty-foot spinning blades, and more were popping up around Costashire and Devnya Town. Spearheaded by Wren's great-aunts, these acts of self-preservation had been running as smoothly as the humans would allow it. Progress was hard when the society was so dead set on stagnation.

The princess was trying her best to put a stop to that, to change her defiant parents' wills. That was what made her so beautiful.

Wren sidestepped around an ox-driven wagon to properly enter the mouth of Fawnfield. The buildings here rose five, six stories high, decorated by merchant signs and pennant flags. Everyone had started their days far earlier than he had. The roads smelled of fresh dough and fresher horse poop. The main roads had been unearthed years back, revealing the hidden pavement underneath, but it was still bad for the horses. The wealthier citizens, ones not born with gills or feathers to make traveling different, rode the animals between cycling bikes and hovering boards.

Laughter broke out above him. Sighing, Wren watched as two hoverboarders flew by, coasting above Fawnfield without a sound from their tech. Forget having an airborne dad, it was the fact Wren didn't have a board that made him insanely jealous of his classmates. He loved stealing Juni's board and soaring high above the angled rooftops. Disconnecting from life and letting the wind take him anywhere in the world—it was why he loved running. He wanted to be free.

Moping, he trudged to a fountain made specifically for brackishborne and splashed the water in his face, making sure to get between his gills. His breed didn't have to stay in water nearly as much as others, but even *that* was becoming a bygone problem. Thanks to those lunarborne who'd come down from the Moon so many years ago, inventions were being made at a rapid pace in Drail. According to Great-Aunt Morgan, in less than a century, waterborne would be freed from their long soaks.

"Wren!"

Blinking back the salty water, Wren craned his neck up. Two haughty hoverboarders were idling in place and waving at him, mocking him.

"Hey!" Wren shut off the public tap and flicked his fanned tail on the ground. They weren't hoverboarders. No, he wouldn't give them such an honorific. More like assholes. Lovey-dovey, pain-in-the-ass assholes.

Alexi and Juniper, two girls too casual for being fifty feet up in the air, stuck out their tongues as they teased Wren from above.

"You're late again!" Alexi called down.

"Where's the surprise there?" Juniper asked with a grin. "Did your mom have to wake you up again?"

"And here I was, about to offer you a ride, but seeing as you have no time management skills..." Giving him the finger, Alexi rode off towards the hills between Fawnfield and Costashire, leaving Wren grounded and red-faced.

"You shitty lovebirds!" He ran off after them, ignoring the soft laughter from the people of Fawnfield watching them. He did his best to evade Great-Aunt Morgan's shop, but it wasn't like she'd actually be there. Her provisional shop was now owned by her son, Vanna, but she and her wife were off getting their grubby hands all over the social fabric of the kingdom. His dad once said that it was Morgan who helped put Fawnfield on the map, along with another girl, a special girl no longer with them.

Girls, girls, *girls*. All of Wren's problems stemmed from girls and it drove him mad the more he thought about it.

Ten minutes. It took him ten minutes to reach the coastal hills. A regular person would've needed half the day and a carriage to match his speeds. Not like anyone here would've praised him for that. They chose to bully him instead.

He caught his breath in a field of dandelions. Behind him were the scattered farms that marked the end of Fawnfield, and down the northern hills was Costashire. The port city floated within the ocean's bay. It was a rather large port city, the biggest one on the coast. Sailors and fisherfolk from all across Drail made it a destination spot for their ships. Giant ships were docked around the waterborne community, and the smell of salt warmed in the breeze. The homes trickled down from the hills and into the water, where the majority of the people lived, submerged and comfortable in their natural habitat.

Wren almost stopped to admire the sight below, if it wasn't for his two most hated people waiting for him by the picnic bench.

Lexi and Juni had made themselves comfortable *around* the wooden bench, because why on Earth would they use a thing the right way? Today, they'd set up their study date on the ground. Spread out around the yellow dune grass were a patchwork quilt, a picnic basket, wrapped cheeses, and loaves of bread sitting atop worn books.

"He finally shows," Juni said, and folded her silver wings to get a better look at Wren. "You're sweaty."

"Oh, am I? I couldn't tell. You could've done me a solid by picking me up, but *no*." Wren sat down on their picnic table and used his fanned tail to cool himself off. The bench wasn't "theirs" per say, but after years of meeting up like this, nobody had told them they *couldn't* claim it. They'd even marked the wood with their initials, scribing ownership to a small part of the world.

Lexi giggled as she handed Wren a glass of water with lemon. The water was too warm for Wren's liking, and he made a note of grimacing at its taste when he finished it. "Also, you know it's not safe to couple-ride on hoverboards."

"You were *just* doing it," he told the girl.

"Well, yeah, but that's because I'm so light and petite." Lexi kicked her leg up like a bratty princess as she used her scaly, sharp tail to drag it along Juni's boots. "Plus, we're in *love*. And couple riding isn't banned yet."

"Gag me," Wren choked.

"Only if you keep whining." Juni sliced up one of the loaves of bread and split a third of it with Wren. "We couldn't get cheddar this time."

"Oh, can this day get any worse?" Wren dramatically put a hand to his forehead as he blindly reached for the bread. Juni kept it from his reach until he had no choice but to reach over the bench and nab it from her. "Ass."

"You love it."

"And you love *us*," Lexi pressed. "Because you're helping us with this stupid project."

"Who says I'm helping you now?"

"You promised! You're older than us. How difficult can it be to help us with our homework?"

"It's not homework, it's your final exam."

"Semantics."

Wren scoffed. "*And* we already got caught this month cheating, and I can't take seeing my mom so sad. Will you knowingly hurt my mom's feelings? If you recall, she helped raise you."

"Who *didn't* help raise me?" Lexi watched the windmills nearest them gently turn in the soft breeze. She stretched, jumping to her tiptoes in excitement. "Where's Emmie? Did you see her coming up from the forest?"

"She never comes out on these dates, you know that," Wren said. "She's in extracurriculars *and* getting tutored by her parents."

"Didn't her mom get hired as the princess' personal nurse?" Juni asked. "She has that lower back condition now. Some say she isn't fit to rule with it."

Wren sliced deep into a piece of hardened cheese. He plopped it into his mouth. "Don't speak ill of the princess like that."

"Yeah, don't speak ill of Wren's *girlfriend*," Lexi teased.

"Shut up!" Wren kicked his boot into the sandy dirt. To say he had a crush on Princess Cellena was like saying someone loved water or air. How couldn't he admire perfection? Tall, with long, silky, black hair. Regal. Elegant. Well-mannered. Kind to crossborne since the day she met one. She was in her twenties now, much older than when her older brother, Jabel, abdicated his right to the throne, but that didn't stop Wren's feelings.

"Besides," he said dismissively, "everyone knows the princess isn't gonna marry some common crossbreed. The monarch's wouldn't let her."

The long dune grass shifted as the air changed in pressure behind them. "That's not what I've heard."

The three of them turned to their missing fourth.

Noemi, a dragonborne with curved horns, levitated up the hill and stopped beside Juni. She walked around the picnic table with her hands folded behind her back, eyeing their breakfast.

"Hi to you, too, Emmie," Wren said.

"Emmie!" Lexi ran up and hugged her from the side, nearly crushing her. Emmie teleported out of her grasp and hovered feet above them, temporarily saved.

"You're so crass," Emmie said. "Don't any of you have manners?"

Lexi mocked Emmie's tone, then tried handing her a piece of bread, waving it near her like a dog with a stick.

Emmie didn't bite. She flipped back her quaffed, dark hair with a know-it-all smile. "Word on the wind says Princess Cellena is looking for a suitor," she told them. "She's coming of age. According to my mother, she already has a list."

"What?" Wren asked. "What list? Where is it?"

"As if she'd actually make a physical one," Juni said. "You're so hopeless, Wren."

Wren sighed and rubbed his back fin against the table as he slid down. "That's so unfair. I just turned of age, too."

"Not all hope is lost," Lexi said, arms out. She hugged herself into a stupid twirl. "Her brother just got married to his dragon boyfriend. Sanctioned and everything. A same-sex marriage to a commoner *and* someone of a different species."

"I was at the wedding," Emmie bragged. "Very beautiful. Cellena was there, too."

"Rub it in, why don't you?" Wren spat. Out of all of them, only Derek, Kevin's twin, had been invited to the wedding. Something about them being friends from before, back when Derek got to the island before the rest of them. They'd wanted the ceremony small in case anyone against them would try and stop it.

"There's still hope for you, is what I'm saying," Lexi said. "She's gonna change the world for the better."

"I know it," Wren said.

After Emmie finally decided to grace their presence by her late arrival, the four friends finally got to work. On the food. Wren would never admit it to their faces, but Lexi and Juni knew how to prepare a meal. The salted butter melted into the plump bread and charred toast, and one of them had picked fresh herbs to sprinkle into the crusts.

Give it up to the two kids raised primarily by robots to know how to be the world's best chefs. Marcos and Yuki, the world's only robots leftover from the Convergence, had thousands of years' worth of recipes inside their robotic minds. Yet another reason why Wren loathed the girls.

They acted like they were so much better than everybody because of it. According to ancient texts and talks from the adults, the world used to have hundreds of robotic people serving the whims of beingkind. Everyone had hoverboards. Crossbreeds once lived across the world. Then...

Things happened. People much more powerful than any monarch had nearly killed them all, Wren's dad included. He and his friends had once been magically connected to divine beings who'd loved them, or hated them, or wanted them in some regard. They would've done anything for them, even kill for them.

But that was a long time ago. His dad didn't like talking about it, but at night, when Wren was supposed to be asleep, he heard things. Whispered in the darkness of his parents' room, his dad would talk about it with his mom. He'd unpack feelings he had about this "Maïmoú" person, about the "Deities" that supposedly once lived.

It wasn't that Wren didn't believe his dad, but how could he say they existed anymore? There was no evidence. You couldn't see them or hear them. They didn't even leave shadows. His dad used to be able to speak with them, but it'd been years, and the aftermath would leave him crying in his mom's arms at night. When that happened, when his dad would be so overcome with loss, Wren went back to his room and acted extra happy at the breakfast table the following morning.

In the end, Wren believed them. He believed them the same way he believed in and respected those who went to church every weekend. Sometimes faith made you cry at night, made you do things you regretted. But sometimes, a lot of the time, it held your hand, guiding you through the good and bad. He believed, personally, that those feelings were real and important to certain folk.

"Come on!"

Wren blinked back to his own life. After dining on most of the drinks and cheese, they'd stubbornly chosen to work on a few problems for the girls' group project, their papers strewn across the table. They had to come up with a speech for an idea to help better the Drail Kingdom and all its people. Each class had their own project details, but even if they were different classes, the four of them always came together. They ate together, played together, the years between them vanishing.

His dad sometimes talked about "strings of fate," these invisible lines that connected people across multiple lives. Whether you were young, poor, continents apart, or neighbors, you'd find your other halves. Dragons used to be like that, or so the stories go. Now, they just fell in love, pure and simple.

But the way his dad talked about it felt different. The air about it was more...magical. Divine. Whenever Wren pressed him on the matter, he'd drop it, saying it was just a belief he held. That gave Wren all the more reason to believe it had something to do with his divine connection with those people.

Wren definitely didn't have that bond with these girls.

They drove him *mad,* every day, each one finding a new way to humiliate or bully him. *Him*, the eldest of the bunch. Why they decided to work as a group was beyond Wren—they all had different ideas, different ways to prepare their thesis.

"It should be the self-regulated water things!" Lexi said, and slapped Juni's wing. "Right, Juni? Didn't they have them back in the day?"

"I wasn't alive, but yes, according to Yuki, they had devices that attached around your neck. But," she said, gently pushing down Lexi's enthusiasm, "shouldn't we work on the quality of airborne life? Or lunar integration? A lot of the people I came down with are still having trouble acclimating."

"Yeah, but that sounds too...sciencey."

Wren and Juni gave her a look.

"And building a device that allows waterborne to breathe *isn't* science?" Wren asked. "Excuse me, *sciencey?*"

"No! It'll be easy. Give me a few days with your great-aunt and we'll make magic happen."

"The population of dragonborne is a great concern, too," Emmie said. "Their numbers are going up thanks to the lunarborne that came down. Two more babies were born this year, but the crown will have to put in more of an effort so our race doesn't die out in a few generations."

"Sounds like you'll have to find a boyfriend soon, Emmie," Lexi said, nudging her butt with her foot. "You gonna start sailing the seas, trying to find someone new? You're growing up fast."

"I'm older than you! All of you, technically! I was a baby for hundreds of years."

"We've been over this! That *so* doesn't count! You were still a baby during that time!"

"An ancient baby," Juni sneered, which made Emmie crumple what few paragraphs Lexi had written out and toss it over the cliff side. Juni had to fly down to retrieve the soggy pieces of paper.

Wren snickered as the three girls teased each other on what to do. He had jotted down a few ideas on life improvement, but every time he thought of one, two more would jump out at him. They needed to increase food production. There wasn't enough lumber to build houses, not unless they exported it from the newly-discovered countries in the east. And that brought to attention the lack of boats. More and more people wanted to explore this new world now that the so-called invisible Barriers had been taken down. There was still so much to do and see and experience.

Crossing his ankles, Wren relaxed on the bench and watched his best friends bicker like children. There was so much to do, and yet he couldn't make himself get up and change. Change would come whether a couple of idiot kids made up paper-thin ideas for progress or not. Life would always be happening. The morning would always come.

Wren looked past them towards the hills. Between the towns, a newly built radio tower was slowly yet surely being built. Wren's great-aunt was, of course, at the helm of the project, desperate to excel Drail into the stars. The tower was only half-erected—with limited resources, it was hard to get it off the ground, and some humans were rejecting the idea of lunarborne space technology being implemented in Drail. They called it an eye sore. They thought it was evil.

But some parts of humanity, crossbreeds, dragonkind, and the lunarborne weren't afraid of progress. Together, they'd been working on it for years, their quest for radio waves far too tantalizing to allow its disappearance. Certain, special cables were missing, Morgan had said, and pieces of critical knowledge had been lost between generations.

Wren, ignoring his friends, watched as a few airborne flew around the top of its tower. Two of them were at the tip, flapping their giant wings as they fiddled with something at its tallest peak. Then there was a spark, a flash, and the airborne fluttered away in shock.

At the top of the tallest pole, Drail's first radio tower blinked once, then twice, its power fully connected.

When Wren saw it for the first time, all four children of Drail abandoned their schoolwork and ran to go see their future.

THANK YOU TO ALL MY KICKSTARTER BACKERS

Abigail Spears
Akeea Fox
Al E
Albert Cua
ALE Cappacetti Rivera
Alex Carpenter
Alexandra Corrsin
Alexandria Jacobs
Amaryllis Quilliou
Andrea Fornero
Andromeda Taylor-Wallace
Arianne B
Audra and Bree
Autumn Rose
Big Homie
BrambleSpiral
Bramwell AH Crocker
Brenna Greenfield
Brianna
Brooks Moses
Caity Manning
Chelsey Keller
Connor Lee
Dakota Smith
Damadorias
DeNelle
Ellen Mellor
Emily P.
Emma
Erisol
EvanDoesStuff
Finch
FoxDenDenizen
Hannah Carter
Hikaru_wins
Hope Higginbotham
I McClure
illusivium
Iris Springz
IronRequiem
Jackson
Jamie
Jennie_Munchkin
Jimbo O.
Jo Morelli
Joshua M Dreher
Katherine Long
Katherine R
Kemone Armstrong
Kit Farmer
Kylie Krones
Leah R. Cruz
Leishycat
Liesbeth Blackwood
Lou

LumineSomnium
Lynnsie Diamond
Maia
Mari <3
Marten van der Leij
McKenna Hubbard
meehaaw
Mikayla Philp
Morgan G.
MythSigh
Nadine Kennedy
Nanija
NanLia
NekoYang
Nisha Hollis
not at all
Olivia Montoya
Pate
Phillip A
Phoenix B.
R. Joseph Snyder
Ray
Reinelle
Ronin1677
rory polanco

Rune Machin
Sam V
Sami Cortez
Sara-Maude B.
Serenity Sersecion
Sergey Kochergan
Silver
Simon
Stuart Butler
Susan S.
Susan Wilson
T.J. Franks
Teagan L.
Tianna J.
toadboyAJ
V Shadow
Vara
Victoria McRae
Victoria P
Wick P. Crow
Wilfredo J. Villafañe Ortiz
You

www.ingramcontent.com/pod-product-compliance
Lightning Source LLC
LaVergne TN
LVHW092054060526
838201LV00047B/1389